C000184500

Micky's Metamorphosis: A Journey of Beauty and Transformation

Alexander Stone

Published by CDH Publishing House, 2023.

MICKY'S METAMORPHOSIS: A JOURNEY OF BEAUTY AND TRANSFORMATION

First edition. February 10, 2023.

Copyright © 2023 Alexander Stone.

ISBN: 979-8215968826

Written by Alexander Stone.

Also by Alexander Stone

Intro

I just finished polishing Shelly's toenails making sure to keep the toes separated with cotton and allowed to dry before putting on a second coat. They were a work of art in bright pink. I made sure the cuticles were pushed back so the polish laid perfect on the nail without and ugly edge on the nail. Of course mine were also the same shade as hers and were done earlier in the afternoon. My fingernails were also perfectly manicured in the same color of varnish with ½ inch curves extending out from each finger. I was so proud of how good my hands and toes looked with perfect a manicure and pedicure. My fingers seemed thinner and very delicate with a perfect manicure. Shelly commented on how good they looked and what I good job I did as I blushed in recognition of my expertise in personal grooming.

I was always expected to wear rubber gloves when I did housework so that my hands would remain soft and supple and that my polish never chipped or wore away. I was expected to change the color every other day too making sure I cared for my hands and feet as if they were something special. I even wore special gloves and socks with rubber linings when I went to bed making sure I moisturized my hands and feet with proper lotions and creams before retiring for the night. Shelly's fetish for smooth hands and feet became my obsession also.

Not only was I supposed to take care of my hands and feet but my entire body (except for my long blonde hair) was to be hair free and moisturized each day (except for my Brazilian) so I was smooth as a babies skin. I spent and hour each morning after showering with flowery lotions while taking extra care of my smooth face and neck. The laser hair removal made it easy for me to keep hairless and not have to shave at all. It used to be such a pain shaving every morning but now I can spend the time making sure I cater to my body. That seems to be my whole goal in life right now, to be the most beautiful creature I can be. Shelly offers her time for charities now to keep herself busy during the day. We are financially secure with our investments, early stock buyout and Shelly's unbelievable buyout and bonus offer from the healthcare system she worked at for 8 years. We will never have to work again. Besides that, we share our home with two others and bills are no problem. I simply take care of the house and make sure I am the best "housewife" and maid I can be.

Oh did I forget to tell you I'm Shelly's husband. Or well I used to be. My name was Steven Turner. Now I'm known as Micky (Michelle to my closest friends and lover). I now possess a beautiful 42D set of perky beauties with very nice sensitive nipples and large areolas. The procedures performed to my body (remove fat and mold my body) has given me a 42-24-38 shape without a corset. Of course I did go through corset training and still like to wear one to make my lovely cleavage really stand out. My boyfriend, no sorry...fiancée, wants me to make sure the investment he made in the new me is well taken care of and kept fit and trim for him to use at any time. I don't have any male plumbing anymore, only a wonderful new pussy. Everything was removed as a result of my stupidity.

How in the world did I ever get to this stage in my life? It's really quite simple. Sit back and enjoy as I tell you my tale.

Part 1

As Steven Turner, Senior VP of sales for a small metalworking company, I was on top of the world. Standing 5'9" and 180 lbs., I was a formidable component in basketball, baseball, softball, soccer, well just name it. I was very competitive and fast. I had risen to VP level in just 8 short years and was well respected among my peers. Shelly and I met in college and fell in love. Shelly is 5'8" and 140 lbs. with a beautiful figure. She is really a knockout too. Soon after graduating we married and moved to Chicago for my new company. I started in sales and was very successful in my job. The financial rewards were great and we moved to the suburbs into a very nice house. Shelly couldn't have children and I never pushed the subject with her. Shelly was an only child and I have a two year younger married sister living in Hawaii. Both our parents had died early and Shelly and I were on our own. Our life was really perfect with no responsibilities other than to each other.

Shelly found a job in healthcare and she also was very successful, no I mean extremely successful in a short period of time. We commuted every day for an hour but really didn't mind the trip by train back into the city. It gave us time to talk every day to and from work. We became best friends, not just lovers or husband and wife. We could tell each other anything that was on our minds without worrying about how each other would feel. No subject was off limits and I would talk with her about women's fashions, the latest hairdo's and so on and she would talk about the golf matches and loved football season. She was a true Bear's fan and I a true Cubby fan. As I said, we were best friends.

The company I worked for was going through some hard financial times. We were trying to compete against the big boys in the industry and there was always pressure to increase sales. We were also prime for a takeover. Well guess what? A Japanese company did have their eye on us and our investors were courted heavily, finally accepting a buyout offer making them very rich. I too was financially rewarded from the stock price and options from the buyout. The bad news was that the new company would integrate into the existing company making many of us redundant. No one knew for sure who would stay or who would be let loose. The problem was the industry was not healthy and jobs were scarce. This was a scary time for all of us.

D-day hit and the entire management level was "fired". Here I was 30 something and no job. Shelly told me not to worry and that we could survive on her salary alone. My pride didn't allow that though and I felt like I betrayed her. We didn't travel together to work and our talks were non-existent. I tried looking for work but wouldn't take a job for less than a third of what I made with my old company. This went on for five months as I slipped into a deep depression. I would sleep in to 10AM, clean up the bedroom and sit and watch TV most of the day. I would take care of the lawn and other basic chores but didn't really have the heart to do anything extra. My weight dropped and I became soft and weak, not the trim, fit body I had when I was working and being active in sports. I withdrew from all my sporting activities including golf and became a major couch potato. Shelly would try and get me to do things and get more active but I felt like a loser and every day without a job proved it.

One day I woke up early just after Shelly had left for the city and told myself that was it. If I had to stay at home, I would make it the best home anyone could imagine. It was like an epiphany. I started cleaning myself up, cleaning each room of the house, tended to the lawn, the flowers and had dinner ready for Shelly when she came home. I felt like I was finally contributing. During my renewal I ordered some vitamins from a TV commercial. They promised revitalization of muscles, greater energy, better stamina, a feeling of wellness and they were all natural from the rainforest in Africa. The company pushing the vitamins was South African and boasted testimonial after testimonial of how good they worked and the successes using the products. Not knowing anything about the drug industry and the typical compounds in the drugs, I trusted their sales pitch and testimonials. As part of the new me I ordered a years supply and soon was taking almost 10 pills of various colors and sizes each day. They really did make a difference in my energy, focus and health in a short period of time. My weight still dropped though and my muscle mass seemed to stabilize even though I was doing more exercises. Oh well, at least I wasn't getting fat. My stamina increased and I felt very healthy from the supplements.

Shelly was really proud of me and commented on how good I looked and how happy she was that I was the old me. My work at home became my life and I didn't have any urge to get back into looking for work or playing sports. I even loved working with the flowers, manicuring the lawn and gardens making sure to have fresh flowers in the house and in our bedroom every day. My cooking skills improved and I was serving gourmet dishes every night. I enjoyed becoming the house husband. I even liked ironing. Yes ironing. I could be exact in my creases and I strived to take every wrinkle out of a garment.

After a few months the fall weather approached forcing me to spend more time inside than out. I made sure the gardens were well tended for the winter. I was going to miss being outside but Chicago winters are cold and everyone stays inside. My work clothes were getting grubby too and I started throwing them out opting for loose shorts and tees in the summer and finally loose sweats and sweaters in the colder season. I would stay in these clothes every day and didn't try on any of my suits or dress clothes for over six months. Shelly came home from work one night and told me that we were invited to a cocktail party. I realized I hadn't been out to a party or even associated with my old friends since being let go. I agreed and that night we looked over my clothes and suits to see what I would wear. I tried on a couple of my old suits but with my losing weight, the waist was too big and the jacket just hung on me. Oddly enough though, my butt seemed tight in the pants. I tried tightening the belt but the pants looked ridiculous with my waist much smaller and my ass sticking out. Shelly said we should go get some new clothes and planned on shopping the next day.

We went to the local mall and tried all the major stores catering to menswear. Forget the suits. They would all have to be taken in and they wouldn't be ready for the party. They would also look odd with how much needed to be altered. Store after store but no success. The clothes just didn't fit right. We finally ended up in a "European" designer store with very stylish clothes for men and women, expensive too. The styles were too androgynous to my liking but Shelly liked them and we could mix and match things to make a set. The shirt she chose was kind of silky and the pants had no pockets but fit pretty well. The best fit all day. She also chose a soft sweater in a light pink color to match the pants and shirt. I guess it was OK, they were "men's" things and her reasoning to match fabrics and colors made perfect sense. She even bought me some silky underwear and thin calf high socks (nylon) so the pants would look trim and fit. The shoes were also very European and could have been worn by a woman. A little higher heel than I liked too but she told me how good they looked with the outfit and I just agreed.

That Friday I cleaned up, made sure my fingernails and hands were clean (Shelly's obsession), dressed myself in my new clothes and got ready for Shelly to come home. I made some canapés and had some wine opened. We shared in her days activities while eating the canapés and savoring the fine wine. She complimented me on my clothes and how stylish I looked. As she passed me in the kitchen she swatted my ass. "My but aren't we getting a little plump in the bottom honey".

Plump, yes I was getting plump but did she have to say it. I looked at her and she came up to me and hugged me saying I looked great and not to worry myself about it. I had time to work it off now that I'd be inside for winter.

I wore the sweater around my neck folding the arms over my shoulder. The colors did really match good and I did feel very stylish. Not many men were wearing casual clothes and about half had on suits. I felt a little out of place but enjoyed the party anyway. Shelly and I left the party and drove home getting home around midnight. She couldn't wait, stripping off her clothes and mine as we made our way to the bedroom. We were both tipsy from all the alcohol and couldn't wait for some sparks to fly. I only had my nylon socks and underwear on and quickly took off my socks. I was about to drop the underwear when she told me to leave them on. She left her bra and panties on too telling me she wanted to feel the two of us together in silky things. I have to tell you, sliding against each other was incredibly sexy and I was harder than I have ever been.

Shelly began to kiss me like a wanton bitch in heat. I could tell she was ready for some major sex. The wine and alcohol removed any inhibitions we had as she ground her body against mine almost dry humping me on the bed. Shelly was in heat and I loved it. She made all the moves and seemed to enjoy rubbing my cock through the nylon undies while kissing me and nibbling on my ears. I laid back enjoying the attention. Shelly lowered her head to my nipples and spent the next half hour driving me absolutely crazy with her sucking and biting. I couldn't take it any more and helped her down to my now swollen cock. She played with me through my nylon undies, stroking and toying with my meat. I was ready to explode at any time as she slid off my undies and removed her too. She came back up and positioned herself over my cock and lowered herself onto me. She was wet from being excited and I slid into her without any trouble. We fucked for what seemed like hours in our usual position as well as some new ones

Shelly came up with. I was in heaven. Then all of a sudden Shelly got off me and moved up to my face. She lowered her pussy down onto my mouth and told me to start eating her out. She never really talked like this before but I was so turned on I just obeyed.

I ate Shelly out licking her inside and out, one lip to another, paying attention to her now swollen clit. She started bucking as I brought her to an orgasm. Shelly has been known to squirt at times and she let herself release into my mouth. The sensation and taste were incredible. She got up and remounted me as I came inside of her in less than a minute. I was floating as we both came down from our high and just laid back enjoying the rush. She slid undies back up on me and put some on her too. We laid in each others arms as we fell into a deep sleep.

We woke the next day with Shelly stroking my ass in the underwear. I was wearing hers and she was wearing mine. We must have had some fun last night as she giggled telling me what a great lay I was. I actually blushed. It was a great time though. My nipples seemed a bit sore though. I wonder what she did last night to make them sore. Oh well, what I remember was fantastic. I got out of bed and noticed how well her panties fit. They didn't pinch me like mine did and the seemed to mold to my ass. I looked in the mirror and Shelly also noticed. "Wow, you look great in those dear. Maybe we have to get some more for you to wear." They did feel good I have to admit. I threw on my robe and went down to fix some coffee. Shelly followed and came up to me rubbing my ass through the robe. She nibbled on my ear and said, "Come on sweet cheeks. Let's forget the coffee. I have something sweet and tasty for you." I turned to her and she took my hand leading me back to the bedroom.

Shelly laid me down and mounted me with her tits matching my chest and her pussy grinding into me. She worked her way down my body kissing me, sucking on my nipples which now were very sensitive and down to my panty covered crotch. She licked me from the outside getting me very aroused and hard. I looked down and could see myself getting hard in her pink panties and got incredibly turned on. She could tell and licked the inside of my thighs while she played with my nipples with her hands. I was in heaven. I felt so excited, so wanted, so, well vulnerable. She pulled my pink panties aside and pulled hers aside too releasing my now hard cock. She licked my up and down getting me moist for insertion. I could feel her lower herself down on me as we began to make passionate love. She laid down on top of me kissing me as she ground her pussy into me forcing my cock deep up inside of her. We climaxed together as she cried out with each thrust. I couldn't believe I could go another round after last night. It just felt so, so good and so, so sexy. We melded together only as lovers can do both orgasming. She finally collapsed onto me exhausted from our love making. I just held her as she nuzzled into me. We dozed off and woke with the sun coming in the window. She kissed me deeply and said, "Now I am ready for some coffee." With that, I got up, put my robe back on. Readjusted my private back into the panties and went to finish the coffee. I came back I the bedroom and she was sitting up against the pillows with a very content smile on her face. "You are one very sexy man dear. You can keep my panties too. I know you loved it as much as I did." I seemed to blush again. Where did all this blushing come from. I never blushed before.

After coffee we got up and showered. Our undies definitely needed some laundering with all that juice between us. I put on my new silky underwear and could tell they didn't fit as good as Shelly's. I slipped on my sweat pants and tee shirt like normal. My nipples were really sore and the rubbing against the cotton fabric began to bug me. I came out to the kitchen finding Shelly reading the newspaper and munching on a bagel. I grabbed a donut as she said, "Better watch out for those carbs dear. Everything will settle in your ass." She was right....less carbs for me. I took a grapefruit and enjoyed my breakfast.

I had some cleanup work in the basement scheduled for Saturday while Shelly went and had a manicure and pedicure. She had a standing

Saturday appointment at a spa for her nails. She was obsessed with how they looked and how well she kept her hands and feet. On Sunday nights I would massage her feet and hands and file some of the rough spots on her feet before applying foot and hand cream. She would then don special gloves and socks designed for these treatments. A nice powder blue color. Kind of reminded me of rubber inside but I guess that's what they are designed for.

Working in the basement was hot and sweaty and my chest was really beginning to bother me. My nipples seemed to be rubbing on my shirt and become very raw. I tried loosening up the tee shirt by stretching it but that just seemed to make the rubbing even worse. I finally had to stop and sit down for a bit. Shelly came home while I was in the kitchen taking a break when I told her I had a little problem. I proceeded to tell her about the rubbing and soreness in my nipples. I felt I could tell her anything and she was genuinely concerned. She asked if I was doing anything different, changed shampoos, changed clothes detergents, anything that might cause a reaction. I couldn't think of anything. I was still taking my vitamins but the soreness didn't start until two weeks ago. I had been taking the vitamins now for over six months.

Shelly went to the bathroom and came back with two large 2 inch band-aids. Here, let's try these. They may help stop the chafing. I took off my shirt as she gasped. "Wow, they look real sore and puffy. Did I do that to you last night?" I nodded and she told me she was sorry. The band-aids should help. I don't have much chest hair so I hoped taking them off wouldn't be a problem. I put the tee shirt back on and the band-aids did make an improvement. A least I could move without them hurting. They still felt puffy though. I finished the work in the basement and had a nice dinner with Shelly. We were both tired from the previous evening and mornings aerobic activities and retired early. I still had the band-aids on because the tee shirt I slept in would still hurt them. We woke up on Sunday morning fresh and ready to start the day.

We had breakfast, showered and got dressed. I removed the band-aids after the shower and felt the soreness return. Boy taking them off hurt too. Shelly was looking at me a little odd when she said. "You know what, Ill bet if you wear a silky top your nipples won't hurt. I'll bet the cotton or the chemicals are bothering you." She went into her closet and came out with a silky camisole. I looked at her and said, "I'm not wearing that, that's for girls." She said, "OK then, suffer Mr. Macho man." I looked back at her and took the cami. I didn't want to hurt again and removing the band-aids hurt more than I expected. I slid the cami over my head and it dropped down over my chest. The silky feel was much nicer and there was no pain. She threw me a button down shirt and told me to put it over the top. Once I buttoned it up you couldn't really tell I had the silky cami on. She then threw me a matching pair of panties to the cami. "Here, you may as well wear the set. I don't want things washed unmatched." She was right, it looked like I'd be wearing the cami until my chest stopped hurting and washing it without the panties would ruin the set. At least it made sense to me at the moment. I put on the panties and they felt like a glove. They fit much better than my old cotton undies or even the new silky men's undies. These seemed to fit me without any bunching or pinching.

I put on some more sweats as she said we were going shopping. Shopping, twice in a week. Oh well, she must need some things.

Off to the mall we went again. Shelly was on a mission while I strolled around the store looking at electronics, tools, you know the drill. I met her checking out and saw a pile of women's lingerie and clothes. She must be ready to work out is all I could think of at the time. I took the backs as we went to the lotion store. She stocked up on foot lotions, hand lotions, body creams, medicated body creams and so on. I grabbed the bags again and she said we were done.

We drove home and I carried in all the purchases. We were in the bedroom when she unpacked the clothing bags. There were three sets of camisoles and panty sets, two very thin bras, and two pastel colored jogging sets, definitely women's though. She folded the camis and panties and began putting them in my underwear drawer. "Hey, what are you doing?" I said. "Well if your going to wear these from no on, I don't want you ruining mine. These should do for a few weeks. I picked up the bra. It read 36nearly A. Shelly was a 38C. Oh no, she got this for me too. The jogging sets too. What was she trying to do to me.

"Hey baby, I know this is a shock to you but we can't have you uncomfortable any more in clothes. They are only clothes. What's the big deal. Here, lets try the bra on. There's no padding or form and no underwire so it won't give you any cleavage. It will just wrap around your chest and protect you nipples. I also thought the jogging suit may fit better too and your things are getting really ratty looking. Here let's try on the bra. Before you try it on though, I have some medicated cream that may help reduce the soreness. I took off my shirt and camisole as she opened one of the creams she bought and started rubbing it on my puffy chest. Id did feel good as she rubbed the cream in, almost a little too good. I was getting goose bumps and tingling down my spine as she brushed her hand across my nipples. The nipples were actually getting hard too as she continued applying the cream. She finished and said, "OK let's try the bra now baby."

She helped me with the bra she showed me how to wrap it around and hook it together, spin it around my body and into place and then put my arms into the straps. I followed her instructions fumbling a bit then got it in place. She helped fit the straps and was pleased how well it fit. She was right, no pushing up or making boobs on me. The soft material did make an immediate improvement in how my chest felt. She told me to put the camisole back on to further help friction with my clothing. Next she threw me the bottoms to the jogging set. I pulled the pants up and they fit great. Snug in the waist and just the right amount of room in the ass. She had me put the top on and it fit perfect too. A little room in the top though where my boobs would be. Oh well, It felt good and fit good too. "There, you look great dear. I had a feeling they fit better. They are just for around the house anyway. No ones going to know." I looked in the mirror and saw me, but in a bunch of girls clothes. The odd thing is, they felt fabulous. I didn't want to show too much enjoyment though.

The weeks seemed to fly by as Shelly fell back into her schedule of work while I tended to the domestic chores in the house. I cleaned every week, did the food shopping, did the laundry taking special care of Shelly's and my lingerie, and did all the cooking. I also found myself enjoying painting floral arrangements in our studio as well as arranging the flowers I cut into beautiful centerpieces. I wore jogging suits every day and even had to order more loose clothing on line. I bought more women's jogging suits, women's exercise sets, and even loose women's khaki's. Men's pant's just didn't seem to fit right anymore. I found that I could wear tees over my camisole and bought some tank tops and other short sleeved tees from Michelle's secret and other women's stores for working around the house. I even liked the bright colors more than the drab grey and blue colors from the men's section. Even with the workouts and increased exercise my ass still remained plump and my chest never seemed to reduce the swelling. By using the bra and camisole though my nipples and tissue didn't chafe anymore. One problem solved. The bra seemed to be getting a bit tight though. I also found that I didn't have to shave every day but every third day. My skin was also very smooth and the little hair I had on my arms and legs seemed finer. I could count the hairs on my chest and liked the way I looked with my tight abs. They weren't that tight now though. Soft and smooth but firm.

My activities also extended out to the neighborhood. I felt comfortable that everyone basically ignored me and didn't see me as a guy in drag but a normal girl. I would even have some fun and wear some makeup and lipstick to complete the illusion. As long as I got cleaned up before Shelly got home it was OK. It was my fun time and I liked faking people out about my gender. I had tried crossdressing when

I was a kid and enjoyed the entire process of making myself look like a girl. The clothes helped with the illusion as did the longer hair. I let it grow because I really didn't want to go and get haircuts anymore and it helped hide me as a man and not some odd shaped freak. I liked long hair anyway so what was the big deal. I would play with teasing it and setting it while Shelly was off at work. No big deal, It was just fun trying new things. I would also venture out and go shopping in the malls and local strip stores. I was usually mistaken for a girl and got a kicjk out of getting people to help me or getting a drink or meal for free. It was just fun to play around without any responsibility.

One day while I was jogging around the block and through the park I saw two guys (teenagers) watching me from a bench. I had to pass them to finish the jog. As I approached them one guy jumped up and blocked my way. The other teen came up behind me and hindered my escape. I was now stuck and felt scared and vulnerable. There it is again, vulnerable. "Hey baby, how about taking care of us. You know.....blow us." I felt disgusted. I was too weak and much smaller than the two of them. I couldn't fight these guys and worried what they would do if they found out I was a man. I blabbered out something about having to get home and my family was waiting. They just laughed at me and pulled me back into the bushes. "You scream and you die" one said.

I was pushed down and one guy lowered himself down onto me and began humping me. He started kissing me as I tried to fight back. "Hey baby, if you don't start acting like a true bitch and please us, we'll really fuck you up. Now start kissing me and show me you like me." I was petrified and couldn't believe I was here ready to kiss another guy and give these two guys blowjobs. The one teen lowered his head and pushed his lips up to mine as he opened my mouth and began frenching me. "Come on baby, show him you like it." I had to kiss him back. I hated every minute. The strange thing is I started to enjoy the kiss. I closed my eyes and just let him have me. I kissed him back frenching him and sucking on his face. Strange thing too is that I wasn't getting hard. Even though I could feel the sexual anxiety and a tickle in my stomach, my member didn't flinch. We must have kissed for 10 minutes when the other pushed his buddy off and started all over with me. My mouth was getting tired as is tongue went down my throat. I kissed him back for all it was worth hoping that they would be satisfied with only kissing. Little did I realize the other had lowered his pants and was stroking himself for a blow job. The kissing stopped and I was pulled up to my knees right in front of a huge cock. Mine was nice but this was a monster. He grabbed my head and hair and forced his cock into my mouth. "Don't bite me or else." He said as I started to take him into my mouth. I could taste the salty flavor of his precum as he pulled my head back and forth. He let me go and I reached up and grabbed the base of his cock and started blowing him myself. I felt a ripple of excitement while feeling disgusted at the same time. They really thought I was a hot chick. I blew him until I could feel him tighten up. "I'm cumming, I'm cumming" is all I heard and then I felt him let a huge load into my mouth. "Swallow it bitch. You better not spill any." I tried my best to take it down in one gulp but there was too much and it started oozing out of my mouth. "Catch it bitch. Lick it up" I heard and I moved my hand to my face to catch the cum. I felt him soften up still holding some of the cum in my mouth. I wiped my face and sucked off my fingers like I was told. I was finally able to swallow the rest of the cum in my mouth and felt so disgusted, so betrayed, so used.

Just when I thought I was done, the other teen came up with his pants down and cock hard and I proceeded to take him into my mouth and blow him. I felt a chill down my spine as I heard him moan, call me his beautiful bitch, and his cum hungry slut. Yes I was all of these things at this moment. I still had my eyes closed as I grabbed his cock and licked and sucked and slurped him up. He came just like the first guy in buckets. This time I could hold him and swallowed every drop without spilling any. He softened up and pulled away pulling his pants back up. I looked at the ground with cum on my mouth, my face and in my hair. I kissed two guys like I liked it. Oddly, there was a sense of sexual excitement and thrill from all that happened. It was over and all I wanted to do was go home. But not just yet. The first guy thought it would be fun if I would give him a rim job. That sickened me even more. How more humiliating could it get. He laid on his back in front of me and ordered me to eat and lick his asshole. I was so beaten I just leaned forward and acted like I was hungrily enjoying his asshole. I licked until he couldn't stand the sensation and pulled away. Now I was a true slut. I had cum all over me and smelled like shit.

They pulled up their pants and ran off leaving me on my knees and in a mess. I tried to fix my hair and straighten myself up. I could only walk back to the house after being so violated. I'm glad they didn't want to fuck me. I would surely be dead if they found out I was really a guy. I reached the house and immediately showered. I could still taste the cum and the guys shit in my mouth. I lingered in the shower for 30 minutes and dried off. I looked at myself and could only cry. I was now a cock sucking whore and slut. What did I do to deserve this? I cleaned up, dressed, made dinner and waited for Shelly to get home. She could never know what happened to me in the park. Just never know.

I woke early and was showering the next morning when Shelly came into the bathroom as I stepped out. Usually she was gone when I showered and she came to an abrupt stop and just looked at me. She put her hand over her mouth and gasped. "You have boobs! And look at your curves and ass. What's happening to you"? I seriously didn't see the huge changes over the past few months but knew my things were getting tighter. I started to tear up as she came up to me and hugged me. "We'll have to get you checked out and see what's wrong. OK? I'll make the appointment with my doctor for Saturday. Now get dressed so we can talk a bit before I go." I dried myself and looked at myself from top to bottom. If you take away my head, I did look like a budding teenager.

When I held up a mirror and looked from behind, my shoulder length hair draped over my shoulders, my narrow waist leading to my now very curvy ass did look like a girl's body. I needed to see a doctor and figure out what was happening.

I had now been out of work for over a year and for all intense and purposes, looked like a pubescent girl, not a 30 something man. Shelly and I drove to the doctor on Saturday morning. I felt so bad she couldn't get a manicure or pedicure. I was upsetting her schedule. The doctor was Shelly's gynecologist. It was the only doctor who could see me in such short notice. We sat in the waiting room as Shelly was called up to the desk. "Are you sure you're in the right office Mrs. Cumming's. This say's Steven Turner but all I see is a girl." Shelly whispered and came back to the seat patting me on my leg. The only clothes I could fit in was a bright pink workout suit with the words "Hot Stuff" on the bottom. I ordered them as a joke for Shelly. My feet were smaller and I could fit into Shelly's pink and white tennis shoes. My hair was pulled back into a ponytail and I wore a baseball hat with my ponytail sticking out the opening to hide my face. My top showed signs of my budding breasts. I now filled the nearly A cup and had to get new bras soon.

We were called into the office and I sat on the examining table with stirrups in place. Shelly sat in a chair waiting for the doctor. The door opened and a woman doctor around 40 walked in. She was dressed in a pink skirt suit with tan nylons, 4" heels, manicured fingernails and made up very beautifully. Her hair was cut in a very reserved style. She sat down and began to ask why we were there. She knew I signed in as Steven but didn't want to jump to any conclusions. After about 10 minutes she asked if it was alright to examine me. I felt embarrassed. I had only undressed in front of Shelly. Shelly held my hand and told me it was all right. I removed my sneakers and pink socks, jogging top, my camisole, my bra, lowered my pants, and removed my panties. She handed me a gown and I pulled it up to my body to hide my breasts. "Take a seat on the table, OK?" I sat back up on the examining table

as she had me lay back. "Now put your feet into these stirrups for me."
I did so and felt so open, so vulnerable. She proceeded to examine
me from head to toe. She probed my butt feeling for my prostate, felt
my testicles, measured my cock and even stroked it to erection while
measuring it's length and size. She paid special attention to my breasts,
massaging them, fondling them, squeezing them and cupping them to
determine size. She felt my glands, measured muscle tone, fat density,
took blood, urine and had me even masturbate in a side restroom to
get a semen sample (little as it was). There was really nothing left to
check. She asked me about my diet, my exercise routine, the past years
history and if I took any medications or supplements. I told her about
the supplements and she wanted Shelly to bring back a sample of all the
pills I was taking.

After an hour she told me I could get dressed. Shelly helped me
and giggled when she saw the bra was too tight for me. I was now a
36B. I dressed and we went to her office. She told us that she thinks
that somehow I was subjected to massive doses of female hormones and
that it was too late to stop the changes. She believed I was chemically
neutered. I was somehow introduced to very strong doses and I should
prepare for the worse. I couldn't believe what I was hearing. It was too
much to comprehend. She would rush the samples and hope to have
word back to us by Monday morning. She told us to go home and try
to relax. It wasn't life threatening but may be life changing.

Shelly and I left and went home. We didn't talk until we got home.
She sat me down on the couch and we discussed what the doctor said,
our alternatives and choices for our future. Shelly knew she couldn't
have children so that wasn't a problem. My body changes would
continue though and we had to figure out how to cope with them and
how we were going to live our lives together. We spent the evening
crying in each others arms, laughing about having to buy a new
wardrobe, being mad that I could be so stupid taking strange drugs, and
sitting silent wondering what was to come next.

Sunday came and went. We basically tried avoiding each other waiting for the results from the tests. Monday morning came and the phone rang at 10AM. It was the doctor. Shelly took the call and I could see her eyes well up as she took a tissue and wiped away the tears. She hung up the phone and took my hand. We sat at the kitchen table as she told me the results. I was truly chemically neutered. My testicles were useless and it was doubtful my male member would ever perform with the hormone regimen I was being recommended to undertake. I had to make some choices that needed to be addressed in the next year. We talked again for hours with more tears. I felt so horrible that I even told her what had happened in the park a week earlier. I felt compelled to tell her everything. She was shocked and in awe. I could tell she was hurt but she paid more attention to me and my feelings at the moment.

I finally held Shelly's hand and told her how sorry I was, how stupid it was for me to take the "vitamins" without asking more questions, and how stupid it was of me not to get help when I first started noticing the changes in my body. She told me it was all right and that we would live together as a couple. I still loved her and she loved me. How was I ever going to be her Steven ever again.

We were asked to meet with the doctor on Friday. Shelly had me make sure I was clean and wore as conservative panties and bra for the doctor's visit. Shelly and I had gone shopping on Wednesday and had me fitted for a new bra. I was a 36B. We purchased some new ones with underwire, padding and a real sexy one from Michelle's Secret. It had a matching panty that Shelly made sure we purchased too. The new bras did fit much better and I now looked like a budding teenager in my clothes. Small but noticeable boobs, yes boobs. I wore a neutral colored jogging suit for our visit not to draw too many looks from the girls in the office.

We entered the office and sat waiting our turn for the doctor. We both went to the examining room and waited for the doctor. She came in and asked to disrobe again and had another thorough examination.

This time she spent a lot of time in my ass saying she needed to evaluate my prostate. I hate to say it but it did feel good. She felt up my now full tits sending a shiver down my spine as she measured and brushed my nipple. I closed my eyes so I wouldn't look like I enjoyed it too much. I could tell Shelly knew what was going on and as I opened my eyes I could see a little smirk on her face. I immediately blushed knowing she caught me.

The doctor just went through the examination drawing more blood, taking another semen sample and some odd tests with my feces. That was something new. She told me to get dressed and meet her in her office again. Shelly helped me with my bra and camisole as I finished dressing. I looked at her and she smiled saying, "It felt pretty good didn't it?" as I looked to the ground blushing again. We finished up and went to the doctor's office. We sat listening to all of the options. She discussed hormone treatments because I wasn't producing any male hormones any more and needed a balance in my system, cosmetic options (face, breast and body) and yes, the final surgery. I was also told to stop taking the "vitamins". Way too much in too short a period of time to even consider. Shelly was listening very close and asked a million questions. I was basically sitting there contemplating my new life and reflecting on my old one. Shelly was given pages and pages of information as we stood up and left the doctor's office.

We drive home quietly as we picked up some things in the grocery store for dinner. I unpacked the things and began fixing dinner as usual. I prepared a nice light meal of chicken breasts, broccoli and a salad. We ate only talking about insignificant things. I cleaned up and joined Shelly in the living room watching TV. I sat on the couch next to her as she reached over and stroked my hair. I looked at her as she said, "Well what should we call you now dear?" I just cried as she held me in her arms. I was going to be a girl, her girl.

After composing myself I could tell Shelly wanted to discuss the new arrangements. She didn't want to change my name too much so we settled on Michelle, Micky for short. Kind of like the movie isn't it? We discussed sleeping arrangements, bathroom things, clothes and closet space, shoe space, and so on and so on until midnight. We avoided the changes that would continue to occur with my body. She shut off the TV and said it was time for bed. I followed her and entered our bedroom where only a short time ago we were making passionate love. She went to dresser and took out a beautiful baby blue babydoll nightie with matching panties. She handed it too me telling me I would look great wearing it to bed. I removed my jogging suit and lingerie and put on the sheer panties and babydoll. It fit perfect with my own boobs filling out the top. Shelly put on a similar babydoll in another color as we climbed into bed. I could feel our bodies meld together as we caressed each other through our finery. She played with my nipples sucking and licking them sending cold shivers down my spine. It was truly a heavenly experience. Shelly was making love to me as a girl, her girlfriend, her lesbian girlfriend. I returned her advances and suckled her tits and finally made love to her orally. Her taste was incredible. She was also enjoying the experience as only two girls can do. We slipped into a restful sleep in each others arms.

We woke to bright sunshine and made love again without any penetration. Sorry, my penetration. Shelly took a vibrator out of the drawer and we played with it for over an hour. She had orgasm after orgasm. I could tell she was pleased. She then lubed the vibrator up and had me lay on some pillows as she slowly and softly probed my ass and slid the vibrator into me. She was very careful and loving and I had, as what I believed, my first orgasm as a girl. It was totally different than a man, ejaculating and getting soft. It lasted for what seemed eternity and the feeling was out of this world. She knew I loved it and she kissed me deeply as we got up, put on silky robes and went to have some breakfast. We talked more about my bodily changes, my female life, men problems like in the park, clothes, etc, etc. etc. We talked until noon when she said it was time to clean up. We showered together as she washed me, playing with my tits and nipples and really treating me like something special. She helped me shave my legs and arm pits and trimmed up my pubes so that I would look better in my panties. I washed her and made her feel like a queen. We dried off as she showed me what astringents, moisturizers and creams I need to apply after my shower. She was very understanding when I looked at her quizzically and asked stupid questions. She helped me with my bra and panties as I did her. I felt so loved and yet everything was so unfamiliar to me. I lived with Shelly for over 10 years now and really didn't know everything she went through to look beautiful for me.

Shelly had me put on one of her cashmere sweater sets and a knee length frilly skirt. She had me put on tan pantyhose too. I felt great in the sweater and skirt and loved the silky fell as the skirt brushed up against my legs. She had me sit in front of the vanity as she worked on my hair, styling it up in a very sexy fluffy style. She then proceeded to work on my face explaining all the products and tools (brushes, pads, etc.) she was using to apply the foundations and makeup. She then outlined my lips and put some lipstick on me. She wouldn't let me watch while she worked and then had me look in the mirror when she was finished. I stood up and was amazed. Steven was no more. A very pretty girl stared back at me looking very stylish in her skirt and sweater. My face looked beautiful. I could tell it was me but I looked beautiful. Shelly was behind me smiling as she hugged my shoulders. My hair was perfect with little tendrils of curled hair falling around each ear. Shelly went to get herself done as I just stood and stared at myself. I tried posing a bit as Shelly let out a few laughs at me. She told me to go find a pair of heels while she finished. I looked in her closet and found a nice white pair with a 4" heel. Shelly told me to try them and see how I walked. They slipped on very easy with the nylons and to tell the truth, they fit great. I was very awkward and had trouble balancing in them though. She told me how to take shorter steps, put one foot in front of the other and sway my ass a little. After a few struts down the hall and my rotund ass helping me sway, I got the drift and seemed to handle the heels well.

Shelly finished and rummaged through her closet for a few minutes. She came back into the bathroom and put a few things into a white purse. She turned and said, "OK Micky, time to introduce you to your new life." With that she took my hand and led me to the kitchen, She handed me "my" purse and told me to look inside see the things a girl needed. She put in lipsticks, powder, lip liner, eye liner, mascara, hair brush, comb, eyelash curler, blush, concealer stick and a few other things I'm sure I would need. Shelly even threw two tampons in my purse. I asked her about them and she said every girl needs protection during her time of the month. I blushed as she told me how they were sued. She even had a wallet in the same color in the purse. She handed me some Kleenex and said that every girl needs some Kleenex just for emergencies. She even sprayed on some perfume behind my ear, on my wrists and behind my knees. I had seen Shelly do this before but just figured she liked the smell. I noticed the flowery scent and knew it was me. I got goose bumps thinking that I smelled just heavenly.

I took my old wallet and transferred my cards and other stuff into my new wallet. I still had all my old cards in the name of Steven. We would have to change everything including my driver's license. Shelly then took my arm and attached a woman's watch, the one I gave to her two years ago. My arm was noticeable smaller and it fit me perfect. The other arm she attached a gold bangle. A fake diamond ring on my right hand and the special present was her set of old wedding rings. I bought her a bigger diamond and new band on our fifth anniversary. She took off my wedding ring and put on her set as a gift to me. They were a little tight but I was so proud being her "husband" at that moment I could have cried. Shelly opened the closet and handed me a light coat. "Hey girlfriend, it's time to go on a shopping trip." Wow shopping again, I guess it's just a girls thing.

We got in the car with her driving and headed off to the mall. Sitting in the car felt odd with my legs open to the air and not covered with pants. She told me how to sit making sure my skirt was smoothed out and adjusted underneath me and how I needed to sit with my legs together. Being a girl was going to take some work. We got to the mall and had the valet park our car. I was advised to swing my legs out slowly so I didn't flash everyone. I stood up and took my purse as Shelly hooked my arm in hers as we strutted off to the stores. We shopped and shopped until I got so tired that me feet couldn't walk any more. She suggested we sit and have a few cocktails. We found a nice bistro and ordered some fancy cocktails. Shelly had a Cosmopolitan and I had the same. I felt so girly, all dressed up and with Shelly.......my wife.

I was getting a bit tipsy when Shelly said it was time to get some special things at Frederick's. I knew Fredericks from buying Shelly some things at Christmas but now it was something different. What did she have in mind? We walked in to a lingerie haven. There were corsets, garters, babydolls, bras, stockings, sex toys, and bustiers all around me in all colors imaginable. We had a ball holding things up and showing off a little. Shelly wanted me to get a beautiful black push up corset with garters, matching panties and silk stockings. I knew my bra size was changing so Shelly suggested I have the sale girl measure me. She wanted a true measurement without the sweater and went into the changing room for a fitting. I removed my sweater and the girl put the tape around me and made a few measurements. She told me to take off my bra and skirt and she would be right back. I quickly took off my bra feeling very naked and took off my skirt hanging it on a hook.

The salesgirl just came back in to the room with her hands full of things. My arms were crossed over my tits. I felt embarrassed revealing my new tits to another girl other than Shelly. She told me to relax, she did this with girls all the time. I lowered my arms and looked down. My tits were very perky and my silver dollar aerole's and nipples were so cute. My nipples were hard too and the salesgirl noticed. She told me to raise my arms as she wrapped the corset around my body. She brushed my nipple sending some tingles through me. I bet she knew it too because I saw a smile on her face. She hooked me into the corset and started pulling on the strings in the back. She said the she would tighten it so that I could get the full effect on my waist and cleavage. I could barely breathe as she pulled tighter on the strings. Finally she said she was all done and I could breathe normal. Normal, that was ridiculous, I could only take short breaths because of the damned thing. What I did notice is than my tits were pushed up very high and I had some major cleavage. I mean major. My B cups looked absolutely phenomenal. The salesgirl was also impressed as she adjusted the garters. "Now how about the panties and the stockings?" I couldn't let her know my secret so I asked her if I could change alone. She looked at me sadly. I think she wanted to see me without panties and try something. She said OK and left the room. I changed panties and my hose putting on the new ones with the sheer black stockings. I couldn't believe how sexy I felt in the new things and with my cleavage showing off to the world. "Are you decent yet dear?" the salesgirl asked as I hurried and adjusted myself in the panties. "I'm done." I said as she hurried into the room. She stood back and whistled, yes whistled. "My, oh my, you are absolutely beautiful. She reached forward and hugged me, our tits touching as she kissed me on the cheek, lingering for a moment. She pulled back but not fully as we stood face to face. I could tell she liked what she saw and I blushed knowing what effect I was having on this girl.

We stood staring for what seemed forever and then it happened. She leaned forward and ever so sweetly and ever so gently kissed me on the lips. My eyes were open the whole time but hers were closed. Her lips were so sweet, so soft, so supple. She pulled her head back, opened her eyes and smiled. I was overwhelmed with feelings at the moment. She reached forward with her hand and placed it on my shoulder. Her other hand gently stroked the tops of my tits which were busting out of the corset. I just stood there confused what was happening. She then dropped one arm and put it behind my back. She beckoned me to come closer to her as our lips met in a more passionate kiss, our tongues dancing with each other and our lipstick meshing with each others. I was getting turned on, really turned on. The little guy downstairs didn't respond at all but I was feeling butterfly's in my stomach and a warmth I'd never felt before overtake me. Our kiss became a struggle for dominance as she kissed my neck, my bosom, and back up to my lips. She nibbled my ears and back to my mouth. All my instincts said no but my emotions let it flow. She even took my hand and guided it down to her love nest pushing me to feel her up and finger her. I knew what to do by being with Shelly but This girl wanted another "girl" to finger her. I stroked her and played with her clit while still embraced in a loving sensual kiss until she shuddered knowing she just had an orgasm. We finally stopped kissing and she nuzzled against me as she stroked my tits. I was hot, out of breath and turned on. The salesgirl looked up at me and smiled in acknowledgement of our lustful exchange. I could tell she enjoyed every minute together. "By the way dear, my name is Stacy. Please come back soon so I can show you some more wonderful things......and lingerie too." She smiled again knowing I too loved every second of our bonding.

I needed to sit. I looked her in the eye and told her I had to sit. She led me to a couch in the changing room where I sat in my new things reflecting on what had just happened. I was hit on by a girl believing I was a real girl. I felt so wanted, so sexy and just so damned confused. She gave me a glass of water and fixed my lipstick that was smudged on my face. She kissed me again gently as she led me to the restroom where I could fix myself up before going back to Shelly.

Before I did I put my sweater and skirt back on over my new things, I put my bra, nylons and undies in a bag, put on my heels and took my purse to fix my makeup. I could smell her sex on my fingers and hand and washed them before fixing myself up. Her aroma was quite sexy though and I was still turned on from what just happened. I did taste my finger before I washed up and was pleased with how sweet her nectar tasted.

Shelly must have wondered what in the world was taking so long. I redid my lip liner, blush, powered myself, reapplied mascara, spritzed on some more perfume on my neck and wrists and straightened my hair. I looked as good as gold. I was ready to reenter reality and go see Shelly. The sweater looked great with my new push up look but the heels had to go. I need a black pair to set everything off.

I came out into the store and Shelly was holding up some dresses. She caught me coming out and came up to me asking what took so long. She winked at me. Yes, she actually winked. What was that, I mean why the wink? She saw my shoes and then my new cleavage. "Wow, you look simply smashing Micky." I blushed again acknowledging the compliment. Those heels have to go though dear and why don't you try on this dress. I think you will look marvelous with your new titties. She called them titties. I never called hers titties before. I took the dress as she handed me a pair of 5" black stilettos. I went in the back room hoping not to meet up again with the salesgirl. I quickly changed into the skimpy dress adjusting it to fit over the corset and realized how much of me now showed. I was almost bare on top. My tits were bursting out of the corset and my legs looked great in the short, tight dress. I looked myself over in the mirror and couldn't believe it was really me. I was a curvy, voluptuous hottie. I put on the new high heels and put my things into the bag, straightened everything and then made my debut to Shelly. Her jaw dropped when I came out. She was speechless. I approached her as she reached out and just hugged me saying I was so beautiful. I felt so sexy right at that moment, so beautiful and just a girl.

Shelly paid for everything and said we had two more stops. The first was the jewelry store where I had three sets of piercings in each ear with two sets of different sized diamonds in the top two holes and one set of dangling gold chandelier earrings in the lower hole. Off to the next stop. Shelly said this was something special. I could feel men staring at us, no me, as we walked through the mall. I felt like eye candy and on display for all the lecherous men. One man even approached us offering to carry our bags. So chivalrous but we declined his offer. I looked up and saw the Forever Spa. This is where Shelly went every Saturday for her manicure and pedicure. She looked at me, smiled and nodded. "Yes dear time to be pampered."

We went in and Shelly was surrounded by three women who took her bags and took her coat. She introduced me as her sister, Micky who was staying with her for a few months. They all giggled and helped me with my things. They commented on my dress, my figure, my hair and looked at my hands. My hands were a real mess. I never took good care of them and I was in desperate need of major work. They told me I would be well taken care of as they led Shelly and me back into the salon. I was entering the inner realm reserved for women. There were side rooms with women getting their eyebrows waxed. One room was designed for leg and bikini waxes, one room for pedicures, manicure stations, hair styling chairs, and everything else to make a woman beautiful. The back rooms were reserved for massages, facials, aromatherapies, mud masks, and so on. I could get a complete makeover but today was just the pedicure and manicure. I was shown to a dressing room with Shelly and asked to remove my dress, heels and stockings and put on a smock. Shelly showed me what to do as we hug up out things and sat in the chairs to have our feet pampered. We were first given a glass of Champagne to relax and our feet were pout into a warm bubbling, soapy tub as we soaked for 15 minutes. I felt so comfortable now after walking around all day in my new heels. Our feet were dried as we were given more champagne. Next came the buffing, the filing, the clipping, the leg massage, the foot reflexology massage and finally the nail preparation and polishing. More champagne was served during the entire process too. Wow, this was really the life. I felt so wonderful. Our toes were separated and we were given slippers to go sit at the manicure station. I sat next to Shelly as they removed our jewelry and rings and our hands and arms were massage, our fingernails soaked, trimmed, cuticles pushed back, and prepared for polish.

Shelly whispered to my manicurist as she told me to sit back for a minute while I looked over at Shelly getting her nails polished. The manicurist came back with a small box and buffed my nails in preparation for some extensions. One by one, each nail was attached with half inch long tips on my new acrylic nails. They were trimmed perfectly and polished with the same color as Shelly's and the same color as my toenails. My hands seemed thinner as the rings were put back on and my watch reattached and the bangle slid up my hand on to my wrist. The rings seemed to go on easier too from the oils and lotions they applied during the manicure. Wow, my hands and feet looked tremendous, just like Shelly's.

As out fingers and toes dried we chit chatted about the day, the clothes and being a girl. I told her how I loved the experience and she told me forget the experience, this was my new life. I better get used to it. Once we were dried we took off the smocks and I put on my stockings and dress making sure not to snag them with my new nails. I adjusted myself, looked in the mirror and saw a gorgeous girl staring back. I couldn't be happier than I was right then. I grabbed my purse and headed out to the front where I met Shelly. She paid for everything as the girls who serviced us came out and gave air kisses to both of us. Air kisses, well I guess that's what girls do.

We walked back through the mall and stopped one more time. I was tired but exhilarated. I also had a little more pronounced sway and wiggle in my new heels and dress. Maybe it was the feeling of sexiness and feminine confidence. Anyway I did feel like I was on top of the world. Shelly took me into the Coach store and picked out a darling purse in black for me. She picked out a new black wallet too for my new purse. I transferred everything into my new purse as we headed out the door. One last stop she said. I thought that was two stops ago. I needed a new coat instead of the white one she gave me when we headed out shopping. She chose a fox fur lined short leather jacket with fur around the arms and neck. It was stunning and it fit great. "Now were done, wasn't it fun?" she asked as we grabbed all the bags and headed out to the valet.

We stood waiting for the valet as he came up and gave me the once over. He was checking me out. Me, Steven, no Micky. I really had to get used to this attention. Our car was brought up and our bags stored in the trunk. "OK gorgeous, where shall we have dinner?" I told Shelly she could choose and off we went.

As we drove off and on the highway Shelly looked aver and me with a smile and asked if Frederick's was fun. I told her it was great and I loved the lingerie. "No dear, was it fun", she said. How did she know? I blushed again and lowered my head a bit and said I loved the experience. "OK Micky, I know all about the salesgirl. Her name is Stacy and she's a dyke. Great store for a dyke now isn't it? She tried hitting on every woman who's ever entered the store and believe me, some of the stories I've heard form my girlfriends get pretty racy. So tell me Micky, how was she?" I looked at Shelly and said. "I don't want you getting mad at me. There was nothing I could do." With that Shelly let out a loud laugh and told me everything was OK. She just wanted to know the juicy stuff. She wasn't mad, jealous, disturbed but saw the humor in it. I proceeded to tell her how I was seduced into kissing and fondling and a little extra fondling of her pussy and clit. She knew I couldn't perform and got a kick out of me turning on a dyke. She was also amazed at how decent I fixed myself when I came back into the store. My makeup was done perfect while my perfume wafted all around me. She was very proud of me, not mentioning how I looked with my new assets.

Part 2

We drove into downtown and stopped right in front of Uno's. The valet opened my door and I swung my legs out like Shelly told me as he took my hand and helped me out of the car. Shelly came around and hooked my arm again as we entered the restaurant. The hostess said our reservations would be ready in 30 minutes and would we like to wait at the bar. Reservations............ Shelly set all this up. We gave our coats to the coat check and sauntered over to the bar.

There was the usual preppy crowd, some older men and some 20ish and 30ish aged men in suits and casual clothes sipping on Martini's. Shelly and I took a table for two at the bar and ordered two Cosmopolitans. I would have preferred a Bombay Sapphire Martini with a twist but she advised me that the Cosmo was a woman's drink. We were ogled many times as we sipped on our drinks when two men in their 30's approached. One looked very casual and one very classy. "How's it going girls?" the casual guy said. Pretty lame pickup line if you ask me. I wondered what was next. "Come here often?" another lame pickup. The classy one said, "Let me guess your blood type. If I do you heave to join us for dinner. If not, we'll leave you alone." Now that was original. "Here give me your arm and I will tell you your type." I was speechless and Shelly urged me to go ahead, what could go wrong. The man took my arm, caressed my forearm, stroked my hand and looked me directly in the eye, "Your skin and hands are so soft my dear. I can tell you are special. Your "A" Positive". I was dumbstruck. How did he know that? He could tell he guessed it from my response. "I'm right aren't I?" as I nodded my head yes. "Settled then, you two beautiful women get to join us for dinner." Shelly was speechless too but grabbed my arm and whispered to me, "This could turn out to be fun" as we walked with our dates to a table.

I was helped to me seat as we were handed menu's. Girl-boy-girl-boy as we sat down for dinner. The guys were making some idle chit chat as Shelly laughed and flirted with the casual gentleman. Dracula kept looking at me and at my chest. I know he wanted some of me, no all of me. He asked me some questions and I gave him short answers not wanting to let the conversation go too far. Our dinner was served and I had trouble finishing my meal. With my new tightened waist and smaller meals I couldn't eat much any more. Small meals throughout the day seemed to satisfy me. No desert but the guys selected a cognac for after dinner. I was feel light headed and asked Shelly to join my in the powder room. We both left as I tinkled and fixed my makeup. Another spritz of perfume and I was perfect. Shelly was giggling at how I was turning on my date and how romantic it was. I wasn't trying to do anything obvious, I just wanted this to end. I was very uncomfortable with the situation.

As we came back to the table the guys had our coats. They had paid the bill and said they were taking us to a club. Now I was scared but Shelly loved the idea and said yes. Our car could be left with Uno's and we could pick it up any time later that evening. So off to one of the jazz clubs the guy's knew. We walked in and everyone was about our age. Mostly couples and mostly dressed in suits and beautiful dresses. We were shown a table and the guys ordered two Cosmo's for us. I really didn't need any more alcohol but my guard was down and I just agreed. After my second drink the guys were getting kind of chummy with us. My date asked me to dance and I looked at Shelly for help. I saw her flirting with her date and she pushed my arm for me to go dance. He helped me up and we walked to the dance floor. It was a slow song and he put his arms around me and pulled me close to him. I could feel my tits being pressed up to his strong chest and also smell the scent of his aftershave. It was the same kind I used as Steven. His hand dropped to my ass several times as he caressed by butt. I tried not to look directly at him but found it impossible as he changed hands as we danced and repositioned himself with me tight in his arms. When the song ended I looked at him and he bent forward and kissed me on my lips. It was a gentle kiss but he lingered licking his lips and tasting my lipstick as he pulled away. I was stunned. I was being hit on and felt so weak to refuse his advances. He leaned forward again and kissed me more passionately, allowing me to respond. My lips parted as his tongue slowly entered my mouth. My tongue met his and we played together right on the dance floor. I broke our kiss and led him back to the table.

I saw Shelly and her beaux kissing too as I grabbed her arm and told her we had to powder our noses. Shelly got up and followed me into the ladies room. "He kissed me right on the dance floor" I said, almost in tears. Shelly looked at me, tipped my head up and said, "But Micky, you are now a beautiful lady. You deserve the attention and love a man can give." I was confused, a little drunk and scared. My feelings were mixed. I loved how I looked, how I carried myself and even loved the kiss. Should I feel this way? Shelly told me to just enjoy it. I would be experiencing a lot more as a woman soon. Just let myself go with the flow. I dabbed the tears from my eyes, fixed my makeup and applied new lipstick and made sure my tits looked nice and juicy. Shelly took my arm as we went back to our dates.

The rest of the evening in the bar was the same. I danced with Gerald (I finally found out his name). He was an investment banker and was loaded. His buddy was Steven, a sportswriter for the Times. We danced, drank and kissed and I let myself take everything in. I knew Gerald wanted more but not tonight. It was time to leave and our dates escorted us back to Uno's where we picked up our car. Shelly and I gave a good night kiss to our beaux's as they got in their car and left. Our car came and I fell into the seat, tired from the day's activities and emotionally spent. I fell asleep before we even got on the highway. The next thing I know is that we were back at our house and Shelly was trying to help me into the house. I made it inside, kicked off my heels and started stripping down on my way into the bedroom. Shelly did the same. All I could do was take off my dress and stockings before I dropped back onto the pillow and fell asleep.

I woke up with a headache and looked around the room. Shelly was already up and had a nice hot cup of coffee next to me on my dresser. I sat up in bed with two pillows behind me trying to remember everything that happened last night. My head hurt too bad to even think so I just laid there in a daze. Shelly came in and said. "Well hello sweety pie, now don't you just look a mess." I felt too bad to even think what she was saying. Shelly gave me some aspirin as I laid in bed another hour collecting my brains. I got up realizing I still was dressed in my corset, all my jewelry, earrings, and my makeup was a smeared mess. My mascara looked like a horror film and my hair was messed up. I definitely wasn't the sexy lady that took Chicago by storm last night. I looked like her worst nightmare.

I could finally function as I asked Shelly to release me from my bindings. I took off my jewelry and stepped into the nice hot shower. I washed my hair and removed as much makeup as would come off in the shower. My body was sore, my feet hurt and my mind was numb from all the things happening to me. I dried off and saw that I did a terrible job on cleaning my face. Just then Shelly came in and told me how to use dreams and makeup removers. I followed her instructions and got myself cleaned up. I had to moisturize then as per her instructions. I put on a regular bra, panties and my good old pink jogging suit as I walked into the kitchen to meet up with Shelly. I sat down and she proceeded to download the events of the evening and what a sexy little one I was for my date. My date, I almost forgot. I could taste his aftershave last night and this morning but thought it was mine.

I looked at my hands and feet and got a tickle form how good they looked. I was regaining more function as Shelly served me an egg and a piece of toast. Two boxes were on the counter from last night. The restaurant packaged up our uneaten meals and put it in the car for us as leftovers. Almost the entire meal for me so we had some good eats for today. Shelly kept describing how proud she was of me, how beautiful I looked, how feminine I acted and what a lousy drunk I was. I looked in the mirror and guess what, I had a hickey on my neck. That Gerald! I was too old for a hickey. Shelly laughed and I saw one on her neck too. I should have been jealous but we were out as girlfriends last night, not husband and wife.

Shelly told me I now had to take better care of my hands and feet and also my skin. We went into the bathroom and she reviewed the entire moisturizing and lotion process I had to perform every day. I would also be with her every Saturday for a pedicure and manicure at the spa. We went back into the bedroom and tidied up. I picked up my dress that I had thrown on the coffee table and put my heels in my closet. My stockings were washed and hung to dry as well as my panties. The corset was going back on according to Shelly. She wanted me to make sure I had all the right curves and corset training would make the difference. So I took off my top and bra and raised my arms. Shelly hooked me back up and began tightening the strings again. How could they get much tighter? She finished and I had trouble breathing again. "Short breaths dear. Remember, short breaths." I slowed my breathing and adjusted to the corset. I put on my jogging top but realized I was pushing out too far and it looked ridiculous. Shelly threw me a pink low Vee neck sweater that fit perfect. Yep my cleavage was popping out for the world to see again. At least we were home.

Shelly and I did a few chores but basically recuperated from last night. Shelly got a call around 3 PM and was quiet as she talked for over an hour. She came in and said Steven wanted to know if we were free next weekend. Gerald and he had tickets to the opera and that they wanted us to dress in formal gowns and be their dates. I couldn't believe Shelly agreed to the date. I shook my head but she said it was all part of being the new me. She proceeded to tell me where we were going, who we would meet, what dinner would be like and what party we would be attending after the opera. It just wasn't the opera. It was Gerald's company's annual customer appreciation event for the Chicago elite and we were going as guests. Now I was getting scared. What would I wear, how would I ever pull it off, what if I froze, what if someone knew me, what if, what if, what if?

Shelly calmed me down and told me Gerald had arranged for a fitting for the two of us at a posh woman's store in downtown. We had to be there tomorrow for our first fitting. This was all to fast and too much. MY mind was troubled and yet excited. I nodded at Shelly as she scurried off to plan out the week. I just sat watching TV pondering on how I ever got into this situation. Shelly was all abuzz with the party and flitted around the house all night. It was time to retire and I had had enough for the day. I put on a long silky gown and popped into bed, of course after I moisturized and lotioned up. Shelly soon followed and we were asleep soon thereafter.

Monday came and I went through the same preparations with lotions and creams and made sure I was perfectly made up for the fitting. I tried setting my hair but needed Shelly's help. I was a mass of curls after she was done. Of course Shelly tied me up tight in my corset and I chose a nice pair of pink panties with flowers and pantyhose. I didn't want to mess around with stockings and garters today. I needed a clean line if I had to try on tight dresses. I wore a short pink skirt with a smoke colored stretchy top. Yes the top showed all of my assets, as usual. My white heels and my white purse for today. A light spring jacket finished the look.

Our appointment for our fitting was scheduled at 11AM. We hurried downtown, parked and walked into the boutique. Inside was beautiful with small love seats and curtained areas. This fitting started off as a showing. We sat and had champagne as dress after dress and gown after gown was introduced to us. We picked out several we thought we liked and then it was time for Shelly and I to be fitted. I removed my skirt and top and stepped out just wearing my hose, panties and corset. The girls absolutely loved how the corset made my figure so feminine. My titties were bursting out over the top as usual. The girls come and told me I had to take off the corset to get a true fitting. I would be wearing another type of bustier that would show off more of my cleavage. More, how could I show more. Oh well. They helped me off with the corset and my breasts seemed to stay pushed up and very, very perky. They were quickly measuring my chest, under my boobs, my shoulders, my torso, my inseam (with and without heels) and so on and so on. I was all measured out. One girl brought over a bustier that seemed open in the front. "I think you'll just love this" she said. I held up my arms as she wrapped it around me, fitting my titties in the open cups while hooking me up in the back. She was absolutely right. My tits were now squeezed together, standing up with very little in the middle of my chest. "This is a new style from Australia my dear and it looks fabulous with the new open front gown's." I felt naked really with nothing covering me from my chin to almost my belly button. The back was also very low allowing me wear a very low cut back. It's almost like I had nothing on underneath.

The women then brought out the gowns and dresses we chose. Shelly looked great in everything. Her figure and beauty made every dress look perfect. I tried on about all the dresses not really liking any of the fits when the last girl brought out the lowest cut dress I could ever imagine. It looked like glistening gold and just flowed as they carried it out. It was truly open down to my navel and down to the curve of my ass. I don't know what would ever hold it in place none the less hold my boobs in place. She told me I would have to use another type of bra that fit under my boobs and sticking to them making them stand up and out without a bra. Some type of invisible bra they told me. I removed the bra I was wearing and the girl put the magic petal lifts on to my boobs. The seemed to attach without any glue and they did lift them perfectly without a bra. I was amazed but went ahead with the fitting. I stepped into the gown as the girls lifted it up and slid my arms through the open sleeves. They zipped up the back up to the bottom of my ass and that was it. I turned to the mirror and gasped. It was the most beautiful gown I had ever seen. I was speechless. Shelly came up to me and told me I looked ravishing. The owner said, "Not many girls can pull this dress off. You have a perfect body for this dress my dear. You will be the hit of the party.

I just stood there looking at myself from side to side, from the back, from the front and every other way I could see myself. The dress reminded me of what Jennifer Lopez wore to one of the awards ceremonies. But I definitely looked better than she did right now. I was hot, truly hot. I didn't want the fitting to end but it had to. I was helped out of the dress and put my boring clothes back on. Shelly helped with the corset but I missed the feeling and sex I exuded in the gown. I was told I need to be back on Thursday afternoon for a final fitting and wear the sexiest undies I could find. Here we go shopping again.

I was excited for the next fitting. Shelly and I stopped at Michelle's Secret and bought a beautiful bikini and garter belt set with the silkiest tan colored stockings they had in the store. The price was ridiculous too but it was truly a special event. Shelly bought herself the same things and bought herself a corset like mine. Oh, she bought another corset for me but only in white. It was getting tough to wear black all the time and I needed to was the corset every now and then. We walked out spending just under $500. The price a girl must pay to be beautiful.

Shelly and I went back to the boutique on Thursday and I was wearing my new purchases. Of course off came the corset and on went the invisible bras. They were like to fig leafs that fit directly below my boobs and somehow made them stand out. I stood on the platform in my new gold 5" stilettos as they brought the gown over and had me step in. They zipped it up again and it fit like a glove. Open down to my ass in the back and to my navel in the front. My chest looked even better than the first fitting. I turned and posed as the girls clapped. Shelly was totally in awe. I did look stunning if I do say so myself. Now I needed my hair done. A new pedicure, manicure, facial and a Brazilian waxing were also on the agenda. I would be the bell of the ball and I wanted to feel it, really feel like something special. I took the dress off as they covered it and told me it would be delivered to our house on Saturday. Shelly was so happy for me but I didn't want her to feel left out. Her dress was also stunning and we would be the best dressed women at the party.

Shelly made the arrangements for all our spa stuff for Saturday morning. I dressed in comfortable jogging suit. Yep I put on the suit with "Hot Stuff" on my ass and just a bra and panties. I was nervous about the Brazilian wax because of my little secret my Shelly told me the girls knew who I was and they would take special care of me. The entire morning was a blur. I was waxed, plucked, prodded, primped, my hair was set and beautifully pulled up into and very feminine, very sexy updo with little curls falling down around my face. My makeup was flawless and the manicure and pedicure were fabulous. Shelly and I matched our color. The waxing hurt more than I thought and the girls were careful tucking me away so I didn't give any secrets away. We finished the pampering at 1PM and went for a light lunch. Just a small salad and sparkling water. I couldn't afford to gain any weight with my new dress.

We got home and the dresses were delivered a half hour later. What I didn't know is one of the girls offered to come to the house and help us dress. I felt like a queen. Shelly and I changed into our sexy panties and garter belts, slid up the silky stocking and attached them to the garters and were ready for the dresses. I was fitted with the petals as Shelly put on her corset. She looked simply scrumptious in her dress. Mine came next. I slid on my heels and stepped into the dress. It was raised and zipped up and I turned to see how I looked. The assistant covered her mouth in awe and Shelly just shook her head. I was truly an angel and looked like the gown was made only for me.

Two small boxes were also delivered in our names. I opened mine and found a stunning set of long diamond earrings, a diamond necklace and also a diamond bracelet. Shelly had the same set in hers. Our dresser helped us on with our new jewels and stood back as we posed in our fabulous clothes. A few sprays of perfume on our necks, wrists and behind our legs and we were about ready. Shelly took the perfume and then sprayed it down my open front between my titties. "There, a little extra for you know who." I blushed knowing I had all the goods in place.

The doorbell rang as we grabbed our purses, put a mink wrap around our shoulders and were escorted to a waiting limo for the ride into the city. Gerald and Steven would meet us at the cocktail party prior to the opera. We sipped champagne as Shelly and I giggled and talked about our gowns, the evening and how we felt. I was getting very nervous and excited to say the least.

We pulled up to the opera hall and were escorted into the party where we met up with Gerald and Steven. Gerald looked very handsome in his formal tuxedo and Steven looked very dashing as well. I could tell Gerald couldn't believe his eyes as I entered the room. The crowd seemed to be hushed as Shelly and I walked over to the guys. I tried being the most feminine creature that ever existed and just flowed across the room to meet my date. Gerald put his arm around me, lightly kissed my lips and introduced us to some of his clients. Shelly was also treated like a queen and Steven looked like a Cheshire cat with a grin on his face the entire evening. He scored but Gerald was the true winner. My dress, my body and I, stole the show. Gerald introduced us to several sports legends I knew from my past as Steven. I shook hands with Mike Ditka, Sammy Sosa, and even Michael Jordan. I was in total awe of them and wanted to swap sports stories but knew my place and had to act demure and ladylike. My hand was kissed many times by all the gentlemen we met. We also got to meet Jim Belushi and Jennifer Lopez. Yes Jennifer Lopez. Jennifer was so sweet and commented on how divine I looked in my gown. I looked divine and Jennifer Lopez told me so. I beamed with joy being complimented on how pretty I looked. I was really getting into being a girl and loved all the attention.

We attended the opera arm and arm with our dates and then off to dinner. The evening was fabulous as we finished dinner and mingled in the reception area with the other quests. It was now after midnight and I was getting tired. It had been a very long, very exciting day for me and Shelly. Gerald and Steven then asked us if we would join them in their room for a nightcap. I was a little leery but Shelly loved the idea and off we went, to the penthouse apartment. We entered the apartment and it was huge, The decorations were all antiques, the furniture very expensive and the bar fully stoked. Gerald proceeded to make us all some cocktails as I looked out over the city. Gerald came up to me and handed me my drink as I turned to him. We clinked glasses and we took a few sips. He set his drink down and took my hand standing right in front of me. "Michelle, you were the most beautiful thing I have ever laid eyes on. You look good enough to eat." I started blushing as usual and fluttered my eyes. He leaned forward and softly kissed my lips as we slowly embraced. Our bodies seemed to intertwine as our lips and tongues made love to each other. His hands caressed my back and down into my dress on my ass. He massaged my ass as we kissed passionately. He moved down to my neck as I stretched my head back giving him full access to my neck and breasts. He reached into my gown and massaged my breast. He could feel the petal and focused on my nipples. I felt all tingly inside. We danced together like this for some time back to kissing and him concentrating on my nipples.

We slowed as he took my hand and led me to the bedroom. Shelly, where was Shelly? I saw one of the side bedroom doors closed and heard some laughs and noise coming from the room. Shelly was already having fun. We entered the other bedroom with a huge king sized bed. It was turned down with big fluffy pillows all over. Champagne was being chilled in a bucket and there was soft music playing in the background. It was very romantic as Gerald led me to the bed and sat me down. He opened the champagne and poured two glasses. As we sipped we just stared at each other. I was getting real nervous now. What if Gerald finds out I have a little penis and I'm a guy? But how could he know right now with me in this phenomenal gown, looking fabulous in my diamonds and makeup. I had to, no wanted to please this man tonight. What was I to do?

Gerald closed the door and came back to the bed sitting down next to me. He stoked my hair and then down my spine giving me chills. He nuzzled into my neck kissing it and nibbling on me. I could tell he was getting hot and I too was getting real turned on. He moved his other hand up into my gown and back to my tit. I felt so feminine in his strong arms. I wanted him badly but needed to keep focused on my wants and desires and keep my secret hidden. We fell back on the bed and embraced as we kissed, our lips locked together and our tongues pleasing each other. My mind wandered as I let him stroke my body, softly caressing it and pulling me tighter to him.

If I didn't do something quick he would have me undressed and in bed where he would find out about me. I laid back as we stopped kissing and I said, "Gerald, I'm sorry but it's my time of the month. I really can't go any further tonight." With that he took my hand and kissed it saying, "That's OK Michelle, I will respect your feelings. I still want you to be with me tonight, is that possible. No sex but I really want to hold you and feel your beautiful body next to mine in bed." I fluttered my eyes feeling so wanted and so adored. "Gerald my dear, I would be honored." To seal the deal I took my purse and reached in taking out my tampon. "Just a few things before I get ready though my dear." I showed him the tampon I just got out of my purse. He just smiled knowing what I needed to do. "I'll be back in a jiffy. You just stay there and get comfortable for me. OK?"

As I went into the bathroom I now thanked Shelly for having me put a few tampons in my purse. Boy did they come in handy tonight. I would love nothing more than top have Gerald make me his girl but tonight wasn't the time for surprises. I played in the bathroom for awhile and had to look like I used the tampon. What do I do. Well, I lubed it up with some petroleum jelly I found and placed it in my ass making sure to use the plunger and pull it out quickly. I now had the tampon in my ass and the string hanging out just like a girl. I deposited the package and plunger in the waste bin and collected myself putting on a fresh coat of lipstick to go see Gerald.

I opened the door and the room was dimly lit. I saw Gerald in the bed with no shirt on. I knew he was undressed too. On the bed was a beautiful long gown for bed. Gerald thought of everything. I picked it up smiling and he told me to hurry up and get ready, he wanted me near him. I hurried back into the bathroom and removed my gown, petals, garter and stocking and dazzling jewelry and slipped the gown over my head. It fit perfect with my titties filling out the cups and my curves making me look like a doll. I didn't have any creams or lotions so I figured what the hell, he'll get me even with my makeup.

I walked back into the room and turned off the bathroom light. I slowly slid over to the bed and leaned down to him giving him a sensuous kiss. "Thank you so much for tonight. I felt like a princess tonight. I love this gown too. He reached up and felt my titties through the fabric. I melted from his touch. You thought of everything didn't you?" He smiled and said, "Not everything Michelle (I loved how he called me Michelle). Nut we'll make up for it soon." I knew exactly what he meant but I needed time to figure out how to break it to him.

"Hey big boy, I can't make love to you tonight but I have other ways to please you," drawing my finger under his chin. He smiled as I slid down under the covers positioning myself in front of him. He pulled back the covers exposing his strong, firm body and now very erect 9 inch penis. I was in awe. He was beautiful If I do say so myself. I never was hung like that. I reached forward with my manicured fingers and wrapped the around his thick cock. I stroked him a bit as he closed his eyes enjoying the feeling. I knew exactly what he wanted and how he wanted to feel, being a guy once. Keeping up the stoking, I lowered my head to the tip of his cock and flicked it with my tongue. I could feel him twitch a bit. I then licked the bulb around and around flicking it again and again. I licked up and down the shaft and cupped his balls licking them and massaging them with my tongue. I worked back up his shaft and licked my lipstick covered lips. My lips went over the tip and I lowered onto his cock taking him into my mouth. My tongue was also caressing the shaft. My actions were slow and deliberate and ever so soft. I held the base of his cock and gave him a long sensuous blow job. He was writhing in ecstasy as I licked and sucked and even deep throated him. I made love to his cock with my mouth and didn't view it as a blow job. It was very sexy, very sensual bonding between two people, two guys really.

We made oral love for over an hour when he began to tense up. I knew what was coming as he started moaning. I held his cock, stroking it and sucking it when he moaned out loud, "I'm cumming." I had heard that before from the guys who basically raped me but from Gerald, I knew I was pleasuring my lover. I felt him tighten up as his cock swelled. I felt a gush of his cum squirt into the back of my throat. I wanted all of him and swallowed the first load, and the second, and the third not dripping any or making any mess. He finally slowed as I licked him clean. I looked up at him as I was licking his shaft and smiled at him. He knew I was falling for him and I knew he was falling for me. When he was cleaned up I rose to my knees in front of him as he beckoned me to come up next to him. I slid up next to my man and kissed him full on the mouth. He didn't pull away and kissed me back with passion. I know he could taste his own cum but he didn't seem to care. We snuggled some more as he played with my tits, sucking on them and playing with them. We fell asleep sometime after 3AM in each others arms.

I woke up with a serving tray being brought into the bedroom by a waiter with coffee, pastries, fresh fruit and juices. He sat it down and said, "Good morning miss. I hope you had a nice sleep." He called me miss. I must look a mess though. I didn't take off my makeup last night. Gerald came into the room and poured me a cup of coffee. He brought it over as I sat up with some pillows behind me. Here beautiful, I know you like coffee. He called me beautiful. I was dreaming and didn't want the dream to end. I sipped on the coffee as he got a cup and sat on the bed next to me. He had on drawstring lounge pants with no shirt. Wow was he ever build and handsome. He also was all mine after last night.

We had coffee, talked a bit, and I told him I had to clean myself up. I got up and went into the bathroom where I found every imaginable cream, lotion, moisturizer, makeup and all the necessary brushes and swabs to make myself look beautiful again. Gerald was so sweet and kind to me. I went out to thank him and there on the bed were three sets of skirts and tops with bras, panties and nylons to match. He had the girls in the boutique come up with some clothes for me to wear and wanted to surprise me. I almost cried and ran up to him wrapping my arms around his neck and kissing him on his lips, his face and his neck. He chuckled and told me to go get beautiful. I scurried into the bathroom and proceeded to shower up, fix my hair and makeup and become as beautiful as I could for my lover. Just then I thought about Shelly, what about Shelly?

After I was ready, I came in and tried on the bra and panty sets and the different skirt and tops sets. I picked a school girl looking outfit that buttoned down in front exposing my beautiful titties. I was getting used to showing myself off and thought , what the hell. I put on some new opened toed sandals. No need for nylons in the outfit. I wanted everyone to see my beautiful pedicure and beautifully polished toenails. I step out into the living area and saw Shelly dressed very similar to me but in a different color. I ran up to her and hugged her. She smiled at me and hugged me back. She knew I had fun last night and so did she. I had a tear in my eye and she dabbed it away saying, "Isn't it great being a woman Micky?" I nodded as she hugged me again. The boys were watching the two of us as we embraced. They could tell we loved each other but not to extent they thought.

We joined the boys at the table as they outlined what plans they had for today. Off to Navy Pier, then lunch, then shopping on Michigan Avenue, then cocktails at a fancy bar, then dinner and then back to the apartment for the evening. I didn't now if we should or not but Shelly assured me everything would be great. We grabbed our jackets and purses and held the boys hands as we were off on an adventure packed day in Chicago.

We had a great time and as we were shopping in Michelle's Secret, Shelly was tapped on the shoulder and turned to see one her best friends, Claudia. I knew Claudia too and saw the two talking. I took Gerald's arm and went to another section of the store to look at the corsets and bustiers. I could tell Gerald was a bit uncomfortable as I held one after another up to me. I loved it and loved the fabrics and colors. Shelly and Steven came up as I looked at Shelly. She lipped something to me as she recommended we check out and head off for some drinks. As we were leaving, Shelly grabbed my arm and said that Claudia was sure she knew one of the girls in the store. In fact she looked very familiar but she couldn't put her finger on it. I could tell from Shelly's concern that the girl was me and Claudia recognized my face. Luckily I was a woman now and Claudia had trouble matching the face with a name.

We went to a very trendy bar on Ohio and had drink after drink. I was getting tipsy again and cuddled next to Gerald as we laughed and talked about last night. I was actually relaxed and was enjoying being a woman. We went to dinner and then back to the boys apartment. Back in the apartment we settled in on the couch and watched a movie. To this day I couldn't tell you what movie because all my attention was on Gerald. His wonderful lips, his strong arms, his firm abs and chest were turning me on. I just focused all my energy on really knowing this man. We kissed, nibbled, laughed and just acted like two lovesick teenagers. Shelly was having the same pleasure with her beaux and he was getting a little friskier too. I could see his hands up her top and under her skirt. She could be heard moaning a bit and I know it wasn't from just feeling comfortable. Shelly and Steven got up and Steven said they were off to bed. Shelly was in for another round of wonderful sex. I only wish I could have the same pleasure. Shelly gave me a wink as she and Steven closed the door to the bedroom.

Gerald suggested I go change into my nightgown and get ready for him. I told him I would do anything for him as I went into the bedroom to get ready. I did my usual removal of makeup, lotions, creams and moisturizers and felt I need to look somewhat sexy by putting on some deep red lipstick. A few spritzes of perfume and my silky nightgown slid over my head and I was ready for my man. I climbed into the bed and fluffed my hair up to look like a sexy bride on her wedding night. Gerald came in and handed me a glass of wine. Here take tow of these two, as he handed me two pills. I didn't think anything about it and took the pills. We sat in bed watching TV and kissing when I started to feel real hot, real anxious, real sexy. The feeling deepened as I pulled Gerald closer, kissing him deeply and passionately. I couldn't get enough of him. The room seemed to be in fast motion as I let him ravage me. I didn't even think of my little secret and really didn't care at the moment. All I wanted was this hunk of a man. Gerald then pushed me down to his cock and I gave him the best blowjob of his life. He came and came and I licked up every drop. He then started pulling up my gown as I feebly tried to stop him. I didn't know how to, I did want him. He then got to my panties and pulled them down. Instead of being amazed, Gerald just reached down and stroked my little dick. He even went down and sucked it trying to get it hard.

Nothing happened but Gerald now knew my secret. He then told me to roll on my stomach on top of two pillows. I complied without any resistance. I felt him massage my back, my ass, my legs and kiss me all over. I was delirious with the effect of the wine and the pills. I even was wiggling my ass in his face and he took out some cream and began rubbing it on my ass and into my crack. I felt him rim my asshole with his finger and then I felt some pressure as he carefully inserted on finger into me. I'm glad I took out the tampon this morning. It would be embarrassing to have a sting hanging out of my ass.

Gerald then got up behind me and reached abound to cup my breasts. I felt him open my ass and felt some more pressure on my bud. I could feel him push harder as I felt him slide into me. I had been playing with Shelly and her toys and knew how it felt but this was different. I felt his head enter me then a little pain as he pushed forward deeper into me. He was so, so hard as I could feel him expand my hole. I moaned from the combination of pain and pleasure. The drugs helped a lot by making me feel enjoyment and relaxing me to take all of him in. Gerald finally was fully in and I could feel his pubic hair on my ass. He then slowly started to move back and forth and in and out, fucking me like he would fuck a real girl. My lover knew about me, who I was and he was now making love to me. I was in seventh heaven. Gerald proceeded to fuck me for over an hour. I would change positions as he commanded and sometimes I would face him with my legs pulled apart as he would thrust himself in and out of my waiting ass. I could feel him grunting as I moaned loudly and let out some screams of pleasure form the fucking I was getting. Finally Gerald tensed up and I felt him cum into me. I also had orgasmed as he was inside me sometime during the session. Not once but a few times. I had multiple orgasms that night. The warm feeling of cum invaded my inner being. I felt so much like a real girl being fucked by her first date. Gerald was it, I knew he was the man for me.

We collapsed in each other arms and kissed very tenderly. I was still in heat but need to rest too. I fell asleep in his arms in a peaceful sleep.

I woke up with Gerald still next to me. My ass was sore and I tried remembering what had happened last evening. All I could remember was coming back to the apartment and waiting for him in bed. I reached down and didn't feel any panties. Oh no, what happened last night? I looked over at Gerald and he was still sleeping. He looked so wonderful, so calm, so, well so manly. I got a tickle in my stomach just thinking about him. I carefully got out of bed and used the toilet to relieve myself. I could feel cum on my ass and in my mouth and figured out he knew my secret. My ass felt so good yet sore. I had my cherry popped by this man. Taking a wash cloth, I rinsed it out and wiped myself to clean up the residue. I then brushed my teeth, fixed my hair a bit, washed my face and put a quick moisturizer on ad went back in to see Gerald. He was sitting up with some coffee and I climbed back into bed. I snuggled up next to him and looked him in the eye. "You know don't you?" I asked. He smiled and nodded as I punched hi in the arm. "You know, you make a better women than any I have ever met. You are beautiful, smart, refined, sophisticated, worldly and mostly one very sexy lady." I blushed the deepest red ever and reached up and kissed him. "Thank you dear, you have made the happiest person in the world. No wait, the happiest woman."

We snuggled for another hour just looking into each others eyes and touching each other like lovesick lovers do. We finally got up and showered together. He played with my little dick some more as I played with his now hard cock. I blew him in the shower and he fingered my ass. We dried ourselves and I put on a silky robe while he put on a pair of gym shorts and tee shirt. We walked into the kitchen to find Shelly and Steven in an embrace. Shelly looked up and saw me. She could tell I had fun last night by the way I was beaming. She took my hand and whispered in my ear. "Did you go all the way Micky?" I smiled and nodded without saying a word. She just hugged me tight and told me she loved me.

We all ate breakfast as the boys told us of our plans for the day. More shopping but in a nice jewelry store, then off to a brunch with some clients, and finally a Cubs baseball game. I loved the Cubs and couldn't wait. Just as yesterday, I had new clothes waiting but they were much sexier than yesterdays. A new corset was also there in the room. I needed Shelly's help lacing it up and loved how I felt again being tightened up in a beautiful woman's garment. This time I wore nylons, a black leather skirt, a very revealing lace top buttoned down to expose my titties, 4" white heels, and to top it off, A diamond ring. Yes a real diamond ring. No! Gerald didn't propose but he could have and I would have accepted.

We didn't talk too much about last night or how he knew I was a man. He treated me like a lady and it didn't seem to matter to him. We had a wonderful time and then returned to their apartment. Shelly said we had to get back to our house and the guys seemed dejected. They arranged for a limo to take us home after we packed up all our new things, our beautiful gowns, our new jewelry and our new lingerie. The guys escorted us down to the waiting limo where we kissed them goodbye. The limo ride home was quiet trip. I didn't talk about anything nor did Shelly. When we got home, we unpacked our new things and settled down in our comfy clothes watching TV. I sat next to Shelly and put my head on her shoulder. She was stroking my head as we stared at the screen. We didn't really have to say much, each of us knew what the other was feeling. We went to bed early after our evening ritual of cleansing and moisturizing.

The next morning I got up, showered, cleansed, moisturized and made myself pretty. Shelly had already gotten up, dressed and gone to work. I took extra time to pamper myself and paid close attention to my new body. Without the corset, my new titties were kind of small but very perky. I loved how my nipples seemed to be hard all the time and circled with beautiful aerola. My body was lean but without the corset, I still didn't have much natural curve. My ass was still plump though, one of the things that did excite me. My skin was now very soft from all the moisturizing and treatments just like any other girls. Without all the foundations I looked like a basic girl without any flare though. I grabbed a push up bra to help me look sexy and a new pair of yellow bikini panties. Being spring I could also wear lighter colored clothes and chose a yellow flaired skirt and a sexy chiffon top. I could see my bra through the fabric. My hair was pulled into a ponytail high on top of my head and I put on my diamond earrings. I felt like a new woman again and looked very cute as I posed in the mirror.

My day was pretty boring just watching TV, the soaps, Oprah, and Jerry. Jerry's theme was transsexuals. I had to admit I looked better than any of the girls on stage. It was afternoon and I wanted to make a wonderful dinner for Shelly when she got home. We had nothing in the house so I decided to shop. I grabbed my purse, put a pair of sandals on and off to the market I went. I browsed the store picking up the basics as well as two steaks, fresh vege's and mine. In the vegetable isle I was ogled by a young man in his twenties. I loved the feeling and the attention. He even came up to me and asked me about the freshness of cucumbers. I know it was his pickup line to talk to me and I flirted with him anyway. I finished my shopping and headed out to the flower store to get a fresh bouquet for my wife Shelly. Yes I still considered her my wife even after the past weekend. I was the only person in the flower shop and a cute man waited on me. He didn't have a ring on (I notice these things now) and he was really, really cute. I fluttered my eyes a few times, played with my skirt and basically flirted with this guy too. I was getting used to this and couldn't stop myself really.

The clerk showed me a few arrangements and I chose one with red roses. Shelly loved red roses. He asked me if I would come in the back to make sure he made the arrangement right. I didn't think anything odd but as he passed me on the way to the back of the store he locked the front door. Maybe he didn't want anyone to steal anything while he was in the back. I followed him down a hall to an arrangement area. There were flowers all over the place and it smelly fantastic. I was lost in the wonderful smells as he beckoned me over to the table. I got closer to him and he turned to me, took my shoulders and began kissing me. I tried to pull way but he held me tight. All I could think of is being raped by the two teens. He pushed his lips to mine and tried opening my mouth with his tongue. This guy was really strong and cute too. I could feel my defenses giving in to this hunk. My fighting waned as I began to enjoy the feel of his lips, his strength and his strong attraction to me. I returned his kisses and we pressed our bodies together more as our mouths battled together and our tongues licked and swapped with each other. I could feel his hands on my ass and my breasts too. To tell you the truth, I was getting hot, very hot. My breathing had increased and my senses were in overload. He was horny too and I could feel his cock poking me as he humped my thigh. We were in a passionate embrace kissing, fondling and petting each other. My mind was reeling as this clerk was making me feel like a wanton woman. He then took my shoulders and pushed me down to the floor. I knew exactly what was next as I undid his belt, lowered his pants and boxers and gazed at a tick, beautiful cock.. My hands went up to him as I wrapped my delicate polished hands around him and stroked him a bit. I could see how my red fingernails intertwined around his cock and got tingly at the sight. I licked the precum off the end of his cock and looked up at him with a smile. My head lowered onto him and I sucked him off in no time. He blew his load within a minute. I wonder if this guy had ever been blown before? He sure was a horny one though. He pulled back and sheepishly pulled up his boxers and pants, fumbling with the belt. I stood up, straightened my skirt and top and excused my self to go to the bathroom. I didn't look too bad really. My hair was still fixed in the ponytail but I had to repair my face a bit and my lipstick. I rinsed out my mouth and used my finger to brush my teeth. He didn't taste too bad really. I was becoming quite the little whore and cocksucker wasn't I. I chuckled to myself thinking a year ago I would be on the other side getting the blow job. Now I'm the little slut.

I walked to the front of the store where he had a gorgeous arrangement waiting. I went to pay and he looked at me with a smile and said it was on the house. I knew why and do did he. Maybe this cocksucking could pay off for me one of these days. At least it did this time. I leaned over and softly kissed his lips leaving a trace of my lipstick on his lips. I saw him lick it. I felt like quite the sexy woman at that moment. I grabbed the arrangement and gave a little extra wiggle as I walked out of the store.

Getting home I prepared dinner, set the flowers on the table and waited with a glass of wine for Shelly to get home. She arrived right on time with some more flowers. She handed them to me. A dozen roses. I almost cried. I loved roses too and I was so taken with her thought. I kissed her and hugged her telling her I loved her. She told me the same as we dabbed the tears from our eyes. "I have something to tell you Michelle, sit down." She never called me Michelle, this must be serious. I was getting worried. "The healthcare system I work at is being bought out. I won't have a job soon. But don't worry." Don't worry, she would she out of work without an income. How would we get by? "Based on my level, stock options, amount of stock, retirement package, bonus, severance and a healthy buyout off, we will never have to worry about money again." I looked at her wondering how she could say that. "Well we can put over $3,000,000 in the bank and use the other million to live on. Wow, $4,000,000! She was right, we'd never have to worry about money. I grabbed her and hugged her tightly kissing her between hugs. We finally calmed down and I had to get dinner ready. I poured her some wine as she watched me cook the steams and fresh vege's. We had a darling dinner as we chatted about the things we could buy, the places we could go and our new life.

Part 3

I cleaned up after dinner as Shelly was on a telephone call. She came into the room after ht e call and told me that she told Steven and the boys wanted to celebrate. I was tired from today but knew Shelly wanted to so we proceeded to primp ourselves for a night out. I didn't know if I could handle any more partying but I'd give it a try. I helped Shelly with her hair and makeup and she with mine. She laced me up in my white corset and I laced her too. My body looked gorgeous again with all the curves in the right place and my titties busting out. I chose a strapless cocktail dress topped in silver and black lace. She wore a red number really showing off her legs and tits too. We put our diamonds on, some perfume, our 5" stilettos and off we went into the city. Shelly drove again as I sat looking out the window. "Hey beautiful, so how was your day?" she asked. "Kind of boring, just watched some TV and did some shopping." I said. "You sure? You looked pretty happy when I came home." I turned to her and then spilled my guts about the guy in the market and the guy I blew in the flower store. Shelly laughed, yes laughed. I thought she would be mad but she said, "You know, you are learning fast about what it's like being a woman. I'm actually proud of you. The best part is you can't get pregnant." With that comment we both started laughing.

We pulled into the apartment building and the valet parked our car. Waiting there were our beaux's standing in front of a limo. I kissed Gerald and Shelly kissed Steven. We climbed in the limo and off to a nice club for dancing and cocktails. We danced the night away. I snuggled to every slow dance with Gerald as Shelly followed. We had a wonderful evening as we returned to their apartment. The guys had early flights so we had to leave. I had a tremendous time with Gerald and he treated me like such a lady. He was a true gentleman. Nothing came up about me our, no my, little secret either.

On the way home I asked Shelly if she knew how Gerald knew I was a guy. She looked at me with a smile and told me that Gerald knew the first night. Somehow he could tell and his comment "I could tell you are special" now made sense. If Gerald didn't like men he didn't show it. "I have to tell you Micky, Gerald asked me about you that night. I told him your were transitioning and were afraid to disclose that you were a man. He understood and we talked a bit about your transition and timetable for the change. He also said he would be very gentle with you and not to worry, he would take vary good care of you." I was now crying and dabbing my eyes with a tissue not to let my mascara run. "He also said that Steven and he were good friends but not bi or gay. I hope you don't mind that I am now sleeping with Steven, Micky. I'd hate for you to feel like I am abandoning you." The openness and truth was overpowering but needed to be brought out. We then talked about my body, my changes, what Gerald would like to see and a possible timeframe for my transition. We got home tired and mentally exhausted as we removed our makeup, clothes, moisturized and put on our skimpy babydolls. We slept in each others arms the entire night.

Shelly didn't have to go back to work at all and we spent the next day making plans and setting up arrangement for the doctor. It was a whirlwind time the next week as I met with doctors, shrinks, and cosmetologists. We pampered ourselves at the spa and had a great time together as girlfriends. We net the guys again one night for dinner but didn't sleep with them. It was just a date. I could tell Shelly and Steven were getting real close too just like I had when I dated and finally married Shelly. I felt like I was losing her as a partner but I was getting her as the closest friend I had ever had. That week we changed all my identification on my license, credit cards and social security. I was now

Michelle Marie Turner. We even visited a lawyer to formalize a divorce on paper. Shelly and I agreed we could no longer be husband and wife. We were entering into a new path in our lives and needed to make sure everything was legal. We could still live together but the formal marriage had to end. The facial surgery for my cheeks, nose and chin as well as some liposuction, breast implants and fat replacement were scheduled for the next week. Gerald wanted me to get 42D's. He loved big tits. How could I refuse. I knew I would love them too.

Boy did I ever regret that surgery, only for pain, not results. It hurt and my face looked like I went ten rounds with Ali right after the surgery and my body hurt from the probing and the implants. Within three weeks though I couldn't believe how feminine I looked. Shelly had cared for me the entire time making sure I was comfortable and got all the medications I needed. I now possessed a narrowed and perky nose, higher cheeks and a thinner chin, a thinner waist, bigger titties and fuller hips. They had also lifted my eyes for that Doe look. With makeup, I looked absolutely beautiful, just like a model. I was absolutely a knockout and a hottie.

In another month I was to go to Canada to get the final change. We had many meetings and discussions about what would happen, what would change and how I would adapt and I was ready. My hot body needed to be complete. The time came and Shelly and I went to the clinic. She was with me throughout process and held my hand the entire time in recovery and my recuperation in the clinic. I had catheters, lines, probes and all sorts of other stuff on my body. In a few days they removed the bandages to evaluate the surgery. I looked and I now possessed a vagina. My male plumbing was gone. I was told I didn't need follow up surgery to improve my looks (make my new pussy pretty with labia, clit, hood and all). The doctor I chose performed the surgery to eliminate follow up labioplasty surgery. He said I had the perfect amount of skin and softness that I would be extremely pleased with the results. In the mean time I was now supposed to work on dialating myself to make sure the cavity would expand and take normal size. Wow what a process that was. Shelly seemed to have fun with the ever increasing sizes of dialators playing with me and my new clit and fingering me too. I was released in a week and went home. I continued dialating myself and felt comfortable with my new look. I healed up vary fast and loved how sensitive I felt. My new pussy was getting ready for it's debut.

I recovered at home with Shelly taking great care of me again. After a few more weeks and daily telephone calls from Gerald, it was time for my unveiling. I had healed enough and the doctor said it was OK to have sex. I was to be careful though. Shelly had bought me new corsets and bras. My old ones were too small now although my waist was smaller but the boobs weren't. I couldn't wait for Gerald to see the new me. He thought I was pretty before but now I was stunning.

We arranged to meet at the apartment on Friday afternoon so we could have cocktails and dinner. The boys didn't have anything planned on Saturday either so Shelly and I planned a little mischief would occur that night. We arranged for our usual spa treatment but this time my waxing would be different. We went shopping of Wednesday and bought beautiful cocktail dresses and silky panties to match. We would both be corseted for the evening. Friday came and we spent four hours in the spa. Waxing, pedicures, manicures, hairdo's, facials, massages, aromotherapy's, and finally evening makeup were the order of the day. Out walked two drop dead gorgeous women ready for the evenings adventure and my hopeful deflowering. We went home and packed an overnight bag for each of us. We knew we would be staying overnight.

The afternoon was spent trying on our lingerie with our dresses. I now had a larger chest than Shelly and she loved how my new titties stuck out in my corset. She sucked on them making me get wet, yes actually wet in my new pussy. I proceeded to make love to her pussy licking her outer lips and flicking her clit making her squeal in delight. She had a mind blowing orgasm just laying back on the bed reeling from the high. I cleaned up again making my face look like a vision in loveliness. We helped each other dress making sure everything was just perfect.

Shelly gave me a present before we left. It was my old wedding band made into a necklace. She wanted me to have it to remember our life together and how we have moved on in a new direction. She also handed me something else, two tampons. I looked at her and just laughed. I needed them now, and panty liners too. We packed our stuff and drove into the city to meet the guy's. Ass usual, we parked in the apartment building and the valet arranged for our bags to be delivered to tier apartment. We were to meet in one of the restaurants on the Chicago River. Shelly and I walked arm and arm, hearing the click, click of our 5" stiletto's on the pavement. We were two hot chicks out to see our guy's. We entered the restaurant and were escorted to the bar. As we approached the bar we heard a round of applause as all the people in the bar turned around welcoming us. The people were Gerald and Steven's close friends, Shelly's friends from work and some of my old friends from the past. I looked in the corner and there was my sister and her husband too. This was too much at one time. All these people, all the clapping, all our friends. All that went through my mind was how did they know. Gerald came up to me and kissed me very softly, I threw my arms around him and cried. He tipped my head back and dried my tears with a tissue telling me I looked beautiful and this was all for me.

The rest of the evening went by in a blur. Shelly had been keeping all her and my friends informed as to what had happened to me and about the new me. My sister was even briefed by Shelly and accepted me now as being Michelle. I was a little nervous though with my brother-in-law. Jim and I used to drink and party together chasing women. The way he looked at me and his stares at my titties kind of creeped me out throughout the evening. I felt as if he was undressing me with his eyes. He was my brother-in-law though and my sister's husband. I needed to stop thinking he was hot for me but I knew otherwise.

Gerald introduced me to all his friends as his girlfriend. They didn't know about the real me and Gerald saw no need to tell them. Only Steven knew who I was and what I had become. The party ended around midnight. I kissed my sister on the cheek and she hugged me for all she could. I knew she loved me before and still loved me now. I gave her husband a quick kiss on the cheek and he returned a sly grin. I'd have to watch out for this one. He seemed a little too friendly. The crowd departed and it was only Gerald and me and Steven and Shelly. We walked back to the apartment and up the elevator laughing and joking about the evening's fun. Gerald had his arm tightly around my waist pulling me close to him. I could feel his strength, his masculine power and the smell of his aftershave turned me on. We walked into the apartment and Gerald immediately turned and kissed me. "Boy have I missed you Michelle." Shelly smiled and she and Steven retired to the bedroom. Gerald and I kissed some more as he checked out the new me. He traced my body with his finger. He softly touched my face noticing how feminine I now looked with the procedures. He then reached down and picked me up off the floor in his arms. I put my arms around his neck as He carried me into the bedroom. He laid me down on the bed and moved up to kiss me again. This time with more feeling, more passion more lust. I returned his kisses as we rolled and pressed our bodies together. He had me stand in front of him as he unzipped my dress letting it fall to the floor. My shoes fell off and I stood looking up at my man. Standing there with my new body and curves, he ran his hands up and down my body, inside my thighs, over my breasts and rubbed my new pussy. I could have died. He stood up and removed his shirt, pants, underwear and socks and helped me lay down in bed next to him. I was a little scared as he positioned me facing him on our sides. He touched my lips and said, "Michelle, you are the most beautiful woman I have ever seen. I love you Michelle. Will you have me?" I reached over and threw may arm around him pulling me to him and kissed him for all it was worth. We stooped kissing as I sat up and removed my panties. "Keep the rest on Michelle, you look ravishing. I laid back down in my corset and stockings as we embraced again. "I'll be gentle my dear," he said as he went down to my pussy and made love to my new friend. I could feel his tongue enter me, lick my labia, play with my new, ultra sensitive clit as I moaned in pleasure. He could tell I was pleased with him and he continued licking me, sucking on my clit, flicking it with his tongue and fingering me as I writhed beneath him with new found sensations.

He continued caressing, fingering and licking me to orgasm. This time it was for real. And another, and another. I could see stars and fireworks as I came. He kissed me back up to my titties and then lowered himself onto me as his cock entered my new pussy. With all the dialations I was ready. I was wet with excitement as he slowly pushed in deeper. He began kissing me as he made love to me. I was hot, wet and getting very stimulated from being taken by this man. I was now complete and his woman. We tried some other positions with me on my stomach, my legs up entering me from the front but I really loved doggy style the best. He could reach around and play with my titties while he fucked me from behind. It was a lot different than being fucked in the ass. I had been deflowered and loved it immensely.

I must have cum at least ten times that evening. Gerald came inside of me and then again later in the evening. I never could do that when I was a man. One shot a night was all I could muster. We collapsed in the bed and kissed our way to sleep.

I woke to Gerald kissing my chest and neck. I had a smile on my face. I loved the attention. He was playing with my new pussy again as I giggled and squirmed at his touch. My body was perfect and now I could please a man, fully. Gerald then reached over off the side table and grabbed a little box. I saw him fumbling but didn't know what he was doing. He rolled back over to me and opened the box. Inside was the biggest diamond ring I had ever seen. It sparkled in the light. I looked up into his eyes and he nodded. My feelings for him were the same as He took my hand and slipped the ring on my left hand. He looked into my eyes and said, "Michelle, you have brought sunshine into my life and beauty into my heart. Would you please be my wife?" I was all flustered and nervous and without hesitation said "Yes, yes my dear. I would be honored to be your wife"

We got out of bed and I washed up quickly. I couldn't wait to tell Shelly the news. I threw on a robe over my corset and stocking I still had on and ran out into the living room. Shelly and Steven were sitting at the table holding hands when I ran up to Shelly and just held the ring out in front of her. She smiled and gave me a girl to girl hug. She started crying on my shoulder, cries of joy not sorrow. I was crying to and Shelly tilted my head up and looked into my eyes saying, "You will make a beautiful bride. May I be your Maid of Honor?" I cried again as we hugged some more. I didn't even know Gerald came into the room but he had been there watching the entire crying episode. He was smiling at how giddy I was and how happy I was to be the next Mrs. Gerald Hamlin. Shelly and I sat down as she held my hand and talked to me quietly. She knew Gerald was going to propose to me. That's why she wanted the divorce papers completed and finalized so I could be happy. This was all for me. She was my biggest supporter throughout the ordeal and now my best girlfriend.

The four of us sat down and agreed that we should sell our house and move in with them. Steven and Shelly were lovers and would be together and I would soon be Mrs. Hamlin.

How my life had changed in such a short period of time. It was really a blur but now we now live in this beautiful penthouse apartment overlooking the Chicago skyline and soon to be married. I have assumed the housewife role. Gerald and Steven used to hire a housekeeper but I convinced them I could do it better. I loved cleaning and cooking and I would just spoil them rotten. Secretly I loved costumes and always wanted to dress up as a frilly maid. Maybe I could get my chance. I did all the chores at our last home and told them I would love to keep up our new home. I had nothing else to do during the day anymore and I would love decorating it and adding feminine touches around the place. Shelly knew I loved it and I was now their "housewife" and "maid". I couldn't wait to get my maids uniform.

Gerald and I and Steven and Shelly got along great and Shelly and I began planning my wedding to Gerald. The guy's were always working and were together a lot after work. They said they had clients to entertain and we believed them. I did trust Gerald and knew he loved me. I couldn't get mad or jealous with him knowing how much we meant to each other.

So this brings me back to the beginning of my story. Shelly and I are spending a quiet night at home doing our finger and toe nails. I was now accustomed to primping Shelly and tending to the household chores. I also paid close attention to myself and didn't try too hard keeping the place clean. We had a housekeeper one day a week for backup.

I convinced Gerald, Shelly and Steven I would be fine. They always knew I had the maid come in afterwards. It was just my way of contributing. I did don a frilly maids uniform and Gerald and Steven got such a kick when they first saw me in it they burst out laughing. Shelly came home soon thereafter and I got the same response. After all the jeering and jokes they told me they loved it and if it made me happy, they would support me. I was thrilled. Now I could get some pink ones and frillier ones and also I loved the hotel maids uniform and be stiff and plain. My sewing skills also helped by tightening up the hem and making me mince all around the apartment like a little bimbo. I was having a great time playing and acting out all my fantasies. It was more like a game being the maid than being a chore. I never really cleaned, I just looked busy. I just minced throughout the day trying to keep busy and humor myself. The maid always made sure the place was cleaned and we became wonderful friends.

Epilogue

Shelly planned a beautiful wedding for me and I now was the new Mrs. Hamlin. All's well that end's well, I guess. Oh, by the way. I still visit that flower shop on a regular basis and Alex has become a very close friend of mine. I've even shared my new body with him. He's such a stud and I am so, so sensitive down there.

Shelly and Steven got engaged and I'm going to be her Maid of Honor. My sister and her husband went back to Hawaii and she divorced him three months later. I guess he was having an affair with a Crossdresser and got caught wearing a bra, panties and hose to work. He was outed, fired, and my sister threw him out of the house. He is now living with his crossdressing lover in a small flat down at the waterfront and working the street for money. I always knew he was trouble and he finally got what he deserved..

My close friends didn't contact me again but I now have new friends, new contacts and love being seen with my new husband all around town. Shelly's friends have totally embraced me and we go shopping, to the movies, to plays and out partying together. I'm just one of the girls I guess.

I guess taking the vitamins was probably the best thing I ever did looking back on the events of the past year and a half. I am now a voluptuous woman with a hunk of a man enjoying sex like rabbits. My ex-wife is now my closest girlfriend and confidant.

In retrospect, I was such a fool for giving up my life, my career and my sex for such a stupid decision. I loved being a man and being able to take a woman and make her love me. I now see the other side and feel comfortable in my skin. I am now a woman with all the right stuff and will never look back.

My how a year and a half can change everything.................

Lightning Source UK Ltd.
Milton Keynes UK
UKHW010711270223
417728UK00001B/160